Two Foxy Holiday Hens
and
One Big Rooster

The Foxy Hen Series

Two Foxy Hens and One Big Rooster is the latest book in the Foxy Hen series.

Previous titles:
The Foxy Hens Go Bump in the Night
The Foxy Statehood Hens and Murder Most Fowl
Chik~Lit For Foxy Hens

Purchase all these books at bookstores or at the publisher's website:

http://www.awocbooks.com

Two Foxy Holiday Hens
and
One Big Rooster

Dusty Richards
Jackie King
Peggy Fielding

Deadly Niche Press

Denton Texas

These are works of fiction. Names, characters, places, and incidents are products of the authors' imagination or are used fictiously and are not to be construed as real. Any resemblance to actual events, locales, organizations, or persons, living or dead, is entirely coincidental.

Deadly Niche Press
An imprint of AWOC.COM Publishing
P.O. Box 2819
Denton, TX 76202

Back by Independence Day © 2009
by Dusty Richards – All Rights Reserved.

Thanksgiving with a Mysterious Stranger © 2009
by Jacqueline King - All Rights Reserved.

The Best of Christmas Flowers © 2009
by Peggy Fielding - All Rights Reserved.

No part of this publication may be reproduced, stored in a retrieval system, or transmitted in any form or by any means, electronic, mechanical, recording or otherwise, without written permission, except in the case of brief quotations embodied in critical articles and reviews.

Manufactured in the United States of America

ISBN: 978-0-937660-57-7

Dedicated with thanks to the wonderful librarians at the Kendall Whittier Library in Tulsa, as well as to all the other wonderful librarians in our world.

Back by Independence Day

Dusty Richards

Dusty Richards is the writer of more than 90 western novels. He is a member of Western Writers of American and to date has won two Spur Awards (more than Louis L'Amour) given out annually by this organization to the best of the best for western writing. Dusty lives with his wife, Pat, outside of Springdale, Arkansas where he continues to turn out some of the best novels in his genre.

Chapter 1

California Hankins took his time and studied all the cobwebs in the corners of the ceiling over the steps. Mrs. Sheets must not ever look up when she stomped up there each morning.

"This is the day you planned to leave, isn't it?" She stood with her arms folded over her ample bosom at the bottom of the staircase.

"Don't go worrying yourself to death. I'll pay you my rent for three weeks and if you can rent it while I ain't here, fine. But I want you to dislodge anyone in there when I get back."

"Why Marshal Hankins, your sheets will be fresh and the room spotless when you return."

"I guess that's why I pay you two-fifty a week for my room and board whether I'm here or not."

Then, as if her age and those extra pounds had miraculously fled her body, she made a girlish smile for him. "You know you are one my favorite boarders."

That was only 'cause she got double rent when he was gone—his and the new guy's money. Her two story boarding facility was one step above the worst flop houses in Fort Smith. And he had no intention of marrying her or any other woman like her, no matter if her powdered face cracked from foolish grinning and split half in two.

She held out her hand. "Your hat, sir?"

"I never intended to wear it in the darn dining room," he said under his breath, stepping past her to put his canvas war-bag out on the porch. Coming back inside, he hung his good hat on the wall peg and followed her.

"You know I dislike firearms worn at meals," she said over her shoulder.

"Where I'm going, you sleep with 'em on."

"But this is hardly the Indian Territory. Mandy, bring Marshal Hankins his breakfast."

"I be keeping it warm for you, Marshal." The tall woman came out of the kitchen with a heaping platter of fried eggs, ham, biscuits, a bowl of gravy. With a big smile she promised to bring him his brown sugar sweetened grits.

"A small going away surprise for him before he rides off into the dangerous Indian Territory to perform his duties as a Deputy U.S. Marshal," Maude announced. The other men around the table set down their utensils and clapped.

Feeling his face heat up at the attention, he nodded to them. "Well, you all can rest assured there ain't no two-bit outlaw or horse thief over there going to get to me."

He picked up his fork in one hand, knife in the other. "I'll be back here in less'n a month for the July Fourth Celebration."

Some nodded in approval and the rest at the table went back to feeding their faces.

The two block walk to Harrigan's Livery after his hardy breakfast was no small effort—must be getting soft or else he'd packed too much in his war-bag this time. He'd harden up fast when he got over in the territory. A few days out there in that rough country would callous him to harsh camp life again.

The hustler met him at the big open doors to the stable and in a rusty whisper said, "There's a New Yawk Reporter waiting for you."

"I ain't got no time for him. Is my team hitched and ready?"

"Sure, like you ordered but I don't think she'll take no for an answer."

"She?" What was Rufus talking about?

Rufus bobbed his head. "Yes, sah. She's a pretty determined acting woman."

"I ain't got time—"

"Marshal Hankins," the woman said, coming out of the office in a divided riding skirt and wearing a man's canvas shirt. He guessed her to be thirty past, reddish brown hair in a bob, not ugly but she wasn't a magazine model either. She had plenty of freckles which kinda looked nice to him. That meant she wasn't covered up with powder and make up like some lady of the night.

"Marshal Hankins, that's who I am. Who are you?" He acted standoffish.

"My name is Gertrude Staunton. You may call me Trudy. I am a reporter for the *New York Times* newspaper and you must know what a vast circulation we have all over the United States of America—"

"Get to the point. I have men waiting on me."

"I intend to go with you on this trip and report on how you arrest these men that will be tried in Judge Parker's court."

"Who said so?"

"Marshal Johnson."

"He never told me nothing. I saw him two days ago."

"Would you like to read his letter written to you?"

"He knows I ain't got time to nursemaid a dude around while I'm arresting those felons."

"Here is the letter, sir." She handed him the envelope.

Official enough looking stationary—*United States Federal Court Western District of Arkansas, Fort Smith, Arkansas.* He opened it, hoping for some relief from taking this freckle-faced female along with him.

Dear Cal,

My superiors in Washington D.C. feel we have nothing to hide and we are to take Miss Staunton with us on routine arrests. It is your turn to take her. See to it that she manages to live through this experience.

Hal Johnson

Chief U. S. Marshal for the western district of Arkansas and the Indian Territory

"You understand it now?" she asked.

"Lady, we're not going on a Sunday school picnic. Why don't you wait and ride with Clell Harris or the Brown brothers? They work around close to Fort Smith." That sounded like a much more reasonable place for her to do her reporting.

"No, I want to see a real lawman in action. You, by reputation, are that man."

Cal removed his hat and scratched his thatch of brown hair. He better do what Chief Marshal Johnson said in the letter. But the others in the posse might back out of going along with a woman. How bad could this day get?

"You can ride a horse?" he asked her.

"Yes. I have one that I rented here."

"You have camping gear?"

"Certainly."

He scowled at her. No telling what that bunch at Harrigan's Stables had charged her to rent some dang nag. "Well, load your gear in the wagon. Just one thing Miss—"

"You can call me Trudy, sir."

He looked at the letter again. "I'll warn you right here. Miss Staunton, we eat what we've got and there ain't no fancy restaurants west of here."

"I will be fine. I have been camping many times."

She didn't understand. Shorty and Horsekiller had the manners of a wild boar, coughing up hockers to spit, then farting during meals. No way could he describe them to her, she'd just have to find out for herself. Worse come to worse, she'd always have her rented horse to ride back on. Damn. He could get into more messes and not even out of Fort Smith yet. This wasn't going to be his day.

She oversaw the boy who loaded her bedroll, a war-bag, and a satchel in his wagon. It was that silly straw hat she wore that he wanted to tell her was inadequate, but hell he'd talked enough. His good saddle horse, Whiskey, was hitched on the tailgate. A fifteen hand high, blood bay gelding made a fine one to ride.

"I'm ready, Marshal Hankins."

He never looked aside at her. Only acknowledged he'd heard her. Once on the spring seat of the green farm wagon he unwrapped the lines and spoke sharply to the two mules, Judy and Jock. Big black mules, probably out of Belgium mares. They both acted as anxious as he felt to get out of there. Holding back on the lines, he undid the brakes.

"Here, Judy! Jock! Get over that foolishness you two and settle down." His hands full of two fresh mules and the clogged Garrison Avenue traffic, he forgot all about the woman reporter and headed west. It was four blocks of a thick mixture of rigs, buggies, impatient beer wagon drivers, horseback riders, a man on foot driving two spooky Jersey cows to God knew where, bicycles, and what all. At the foot of Garrison Avenue, he reined up in line for his turn to board the ferry and he set the brakes.

Where was Miss Staunton? The more he looked around the more upset he became—where was that woman? Then he heard her "yoo-hoo" to him from down the street.

He saw the hatless reporter riding a lathered brown horse. She looked even more unraveled when she reined him in beside his rig.

"Where's your hat? What happened?"

"When we went in the street, he wanted to go east." She swept the hair back from her face. "Then he bucked when I tried to turn him. He does that quite well."

"He throw you?"

"Of course not, but I lost my hat and before I could get off and recover it, a large wagon smashed it in a fresh pile of horse apples. I decided I had no use for it any longer."

He climbed down. "We've got to find you a hat. You'll bake to a crisp in this sun."

A wagon freshly unloaded off the ferry was coming up the ramp. He recognized Pete Hancock. He stepped out and waved him down. "Pete, I need a favor."

"What's that, Cal?"

"Sell me your hat?"

Pete took off his wide brimmed felt hat and admired the weather beaten, sweat stained prize.

"I'll take three dollars for it."

"Two."

"That ain't enough. Besides you've got a good hat I'd trade for it and give you two to boot."

Cal looked up. The ferry was loading and he was next. He snatched the hat out of Pete's hands and dug deep in his canvas pants pockets, paid him three dollars, tossed the hat in the wagon and climbed on the seat.

"Any time," Pete said, going on. "Anytime you need a hat just stop me."

"Go to hell. Here Judy! Jock! Get around here." Their hooves thundered onto the hollow ferry as they clamored on board. Brake locked, he looked back. She was trying to lead her horse onto the ferry and the animal was having head slinging fits trying to go backwards. He jumped down and ran in her direction. Going past her, he said, "Watch out. He's going to load, sister."

Beating on the wild eyed horse's butt with his own hat had no positive result. Finally a big strapping boy came by and held his arms like a cradle. Cal, mad to the bone at the worthless animal, agreed. They joined hands under his butt and physically threw the horse onto the deck.

"Thanks," Cal said. Nodding to the waiting ferry man who was smoking a cob pipe, "We're ready."

"I see that Marshal. I see that. I must say I need the two of you around here on a regular basis. That was the swiftest loading of a balky animal I seen in ages."

"Good. Let's go to the Indian Territory."

"Thanks, Marshal Hankins," she started by holding Spook's reins close up with both hands.

"Maybe you ought to let him jump in the river. He'd only do it once."

"Really?"

"Yes. The catfish would enjoy him."

Trudy made a face of disapproval at him before she went on. "I suppose you bought that hat back there for me?"

He turned toward her as the paddle wheel on the ferry's tug began throwing water. "Yes, but I've got to fix it first," he shouted over the noise and went back to his team.

When the ferry docked and the deck hands tied it down, he drove Judy and Jock off it. Looking back, he saw her mount Spooky and when he came to the edge of the barge the gelding soared way out on the cross tie road that led up the sandy bank. She did a good job of keeping her seat in that postage stamp saddle. He nodded and then he drove his mules up the ramp.

Shanty Town belonged to the dregs of Fort Smith's society. Dug outs, unchinked log cabins, ragged tents, and shelters built from crates, even a few hide covered lodges lined the western side of the Arkansas River. He looked around for his men through the trees. They should be coming.

Brake lever set, reins tied, he lifted the tarp covering the contents and found his war-bag. From it, he extracted some long leather lacing, made a hole with his large knife on opposite sides of the brim beside the crown. He looked up for sight of his posse men before he began threading the hat string on her new three dollar sombrero. *Where were those two?*

"Here. Now tie this under your chin and it will only go back on your shoulders when the wind blows it off." He handed it off to Miss Staunton, getting madder by the minute. *Where were those two at?* That camp was scattered down through the sycamore and walnut trees for a mile. And enough Indian dogs in there to bite you a dozen times. Their owners needed to eat more of them. Course the ones that served dog at meals mainly ate milk fat puppies. He never cared for the taste of 'em. *Where were his posse men?*

"They're coming," he said to her, finally seeing Shorty Broyles leading two horses and Christian Horsekiller riding one of them. He must still be drunk from the night before. She was busy adjusting the new hat on her head and she nodded in approval.

Cal dropped off the seat, stepped over the side and hit the ground. Shorty could drive those mules. He'd ride Whiskey.

"You fellows going to come along?" he shouted at Shorty.

"Sure Cal. Chief stayed out late last night with some old— Who in the hell is she?" Shorty must have caught sight of Miss Staunton. The little man was too bowlegged to ever trap a hawg in a corner. He stood 5-4, in cowboy boots. But he could fight a buzz saw, shoot the eyes out of a lizard, and he made a great posse member.

Horsekiller, who Shorty called Chief, appeared wobbly in the saddle. He still looked pretty rough under his unblocked hat and eagle feathers, long braids and wrinkled clothes he'd not worn much over six weeks since they'd last been washed.

"That's Miss Staunton. Marshal Johnson sent her along with us. She's a New York reporter." He emphasized heavy on the Marshal Johnson part.

"She just riding out a ways with us?" Shorty asked like he couldn't believe their assignment included her going with them.

"Nope. She says she's going all the way out and back with us. Going to make us famous I guess, if they print her story."

"Sounds different to me." Shorty hitched both of their horses to the tailgate. "Chief, you–you want to ride in the wagon or ride that horse?"

"Me ride horse."

"All right, you can fall off on your pointed head, but don't cry to me."

"Me no fall off horse. Me Choctaw."

"I don't care what tribe you belong to. You'll fall off." Shorty clapped his hands together then climbed the wagon wheel up to the spring seat.

"We're ready to leave," Cal said to her and motioned to the main road that led westward through the cotton fields filling the bottom land. With a nod she joined him on Spook and they rode side by side.

"Marshal, have you ever been married?" She had a pencil and paper.

"No ma'am, never wanted a wife." Twisted in the saddle, he made sure Shorty was coming with the mules and his rig before he turned back.

"Oh."

"See Miss Staunton, I left home at fifteen to fight in the war and after that I did law work. Neither one's a good job to have a wife to worry about."

"But don't you want to have a wife and family?"

He looked pained at her. "No."

She shrugged. "Where were you raised?"

"Texas, east of Dallas."

"On a farm?'

"Yes."

"What did you raise?"

"Cotton for cash, corn to feed the hawgs and make bread. Listen to them guys out there hoeing and singing in the cotton fields."

"Swing low, sweet chariot—" Their voices in such harmony were like a choir in a big church. The sound carried out to them on the hot dusty road.

"You belong to a church?" she asked.

"I was baptized when I was fourteen."

"What church was that?"

"Baptist, I reckon."

"Do you attend church?"

He looked over at her pained. "Mrs. Staunton. What does my church affiliation have to do with your story about us arresting lawbreakers in the Indian Territory?"

"The man you work for, Federal Judge Isaac Parker, has been portrayed in the press as the devil himself over his hanging so many men. Since you work for him I suspect people back east will think any employee of Parker's must be the devil's workers."

"We are. We are. Let's trot. Them mules are settled enough. We've got to get on with the devil's work. Shorty, rattle their hocks."

"Will the Indian be able to ride at a trot?' She looked shocked by his actions.

"He may have to learn how," he said and set Whiskey into the faster pace. Calling Judge Parker the devil himself—those people back east had no idea the riff-raff and trash they dealt with west of Fort Smith—but she'd soon learn probably more than she wanted to know about them.

Chapter 2

Muskogee was never a peaceful place. They killed town marshals like some towns killed stray dogs. Cal hoped when they arrived in the small town that Waco Burns was still on the job. He had a warrant for the arrest of Simon Barton. It was one of those warrants with three small dots in a row made by a pencil on the outside fold. That meant the prosecutor or Marshal Johnson considered Barton armed and dangerous. Being familiar with everyone around there, Waco might know his whereabouts and his threat.

"Hold up, Shorty," he said and dismounted. He handed his reins to her to hold. The building marked Muskogee Jail was a shotgun building built of raw lumber. It sat half way between a new red brick building on each corner of the near empty block. The town was all laid out in the waving blue stem grass but mostly populated by faded survey stakes.

Cal went inside and could smell the usual jail house stench of urine, fecal odors and dirty socks. The man with his feet on the desk in the front office was not Waco Burns.

"Where's Burns at?" Cal asked.

"He ain't the law here no more. City council fired him two weeks ago and hired me."

"I'm Cal Hankins, U. S. Deputy Marshal. I was hoping Waco was still here. What did he do to get himself fired?"

The man dropped his low top shoes to the floor and rubbed his palms on his pants tops. "My name's Hiram Steppe. As for Waco, the Mayor discovered him in his bed when he returned home early one night from business. Need I say more?"

"No, but it don't sound like a good excuse to fire a man over. Help me out. I have a warrant for one Simon Barton. Word is that he's tough."

"Only man I'd know in this territory any tougher than Barton is Sam Starr."

"I know Starr too. Now where do I find Barton?"

"He's got a place up north on Dyer Crick. Take the Kansas Road and stop at the first store up there. They can tell you where he's at."

"Good. I could use a couple of good posse men to go along to back me up."

"I could use the money, but I can't go. Got to marshal the town."

Cal nodded. Wasn't a helluva lot for a Marshal to do in the daytime unless two black eared jack rabbits got in a fight and he had to separate 'em. But Steppe's reply told him how tough Barton might be to arrest.

"I have a list of names that we have warrants for. You may be holding some of these men in your jail."

"I doubt it. I've got Leroy Harris. He's black. Colby McEntosh and Stormer Cane are back there."

Cal went over the names on his warrant—none matched. He thanked the new lawman as he left the office.

"Do any good in there?" Shorty shouted at him when he came outside.

"No, they fired Waco. A man called Steppe is the new law here."

Shorty scowled at Cal's answer. "Why did they fire Waco."

"For sleeping on the job."

"Sleeping on the job?"

Cal unhitched his horse. "Trouble was it was with the Mayor's wife."

Shorty laughed and Cal swore Miss Staunton's face turned red when he looked over for a response from her over the firing.

"We still going after him?" Shorty asked.

"Let's get him out of the way. What do you think Chief?"

Recovered from his drunk but not his hangover, the chief nodded, "You plenty good man. We can get him."

"So now this man we are going after robbed two men and shot them?" she asked in a guarded voice, riding in close to him.

"Yeah, he got seven dollars, a pocket watch that had a busted main spring and stole one of their horses. The other horse and his own broke loose when he went to shooting them. Bob, the oldest victim and least shot up brother, finally caught his own horse and rode to the agency for help. But his brother, Hugo Shannon, was already dead when they got back to him."

"And Judge Parker will try him?" she asked, pushing her horse in closer.

"And if a jury finds him guilty, Judge Parker will no doubt sentence him to hang."

She shrugged. "He probably needs it then."

"I been telling you these scoundrels that eventually get to his court have usually done a lot more crimes than they ever will be tried for." He led the way for the Kansas Road.

It was near noon time after getting directions at a cross roads store when they reached Simon Barton's place. Cal made her stay out by the road where they parked the wagon. Horsekiller, Shorty and Cal rode up the lane lined with rail fences and grown up in wild plums.

Cal dismounted before the house and a woman came out. She was dressed in a wash worn dress and looked Indian.

"Ma'am, I'm a deputy U.S. Marshal and I am here looking for Simon Barton."

She folded her arms over her flat chest. "He is not here."

"Where did he go?"

She shook her head then rearranged her long hair. "He never tells me."

"Then with your permission we can look in the house and barn for any sign of him."

"I say he is not here!"

"That's what I mean. I won't find him by looking around then, will I?"

"He is not here."

Cal figured that she said the last in a lower tone because she'd already warned Barton to hide better. He raised his left hand and waved for the others to search the place.

"Now if you will let me inside—"

She blocked his way and he pushed her aside with his left arm to gain entrance with his pistol in his right fist. "Barton come out. Hands high."

He eased back toward the kitchen. No sign, no sound, no movement to his command. The man could be anywhere. In a closet. A root cellar. Under a bed. This was when his job got seriously dangerous. A cornered man would show lots of fight.

The woman stood with her arms folded, standing in the main room—sulking.

"Lady, you better tell him to surrender if you want to see him alive."

She acted like a cigar store Indian and ignored him.

"Marshal. Marshal," Shorty called. "We got him."

Thank God. Cal holstered his gun and went outside.

Handcuffed and driven by his two posse men, Barton looked like a pile of straw. Still covered in lots of stems, obviously he'd buried himself in a hay stack. They drove him ahead of them.

At the wagon, Miss Staunton looked the prisoner over. "But he has no shoes."

"Guess we got him up early and he had no time to put them on," Cal said, not worried about the man's feet.

"Won't he need them?"

Shorty used a ten foot chain locked in an iron ring on the back of the wagon and then he locked the other end to the man's cuffs. "Fall down, you can holler."

Barton grumbled something Cal couldn't hear and Shorty climbed back on the seat to drive.

"Isn't that rather inhumane leading this man behind the wagon?" she asked Cal.

"Mrs. Staunton—"

"Miss, marshal."

"Miss Staunton, I assure you that the exercise that Barton will receive this afternoon will make him a better prisoner."

"Marshal, are you expecting trouble from him?"

"I do."

Chasing her horse around in a circle to remount him, she asked "What can he possibly do handcuffed?"

"Kill you."

"I must report in my article I find this form of arrest as unusually severe."

"Severe is when he kills you or injures one of us. You do your job and I'll do mine."

"May I interview him later?"

"Fine, but keep a distance. That man is a killer. Excuse me. I have to ride up and catch the Chief." *Unusually severe*—she had lots to learn about justice in the Nations. Beside the Chief and his horse, Cal lowered his voice, "Joe Highgate lives around here. We have warrants on him for making bad whiskey."

"Any he made would be bad. Might have his socks in it too," the Chief laughed as if considering the matter.

"How far away is Highgate's place?"

"Mud Creek – we can cut across on this next road, maybe two miles."

"Maybe five?" Cal doubted the man's idea of distance.

"Some are Indian miles and they are longer than yours."

There was no way to get ahead of the chief. "Good. We'll arrest him next."

"Excuse me Marshal, who is next on your list?" she asked, riding up on them.

"Joe Highgate. Moonshiner."

"Will he be less dangerous than Barton?"

"No, ma'am. These men are all outlaws. That means they live outside the law. They murder, rape, steal and plunder. Sometimes it is the least offence that we can arrest them for and remove them from the population."

"Is there no law but you out here?"

"There is Indian law on their land, but they can only try Indians. There are Indians who do crimes to white folks and white folks that do things to Indians and other white men. Those crimes are the ones that we must work."

"Barton looks weary back there." She gave a head toss at the prisoner behind the wagon pulled by the jogging mules.

"He ever falls down Shorty will stop."

Before they made Mud Creek, Barton was ready to confess—if only they'd allow him to ride in the wagon. His howling brought Cal back there.

"Did you shoot and rob those two men?" Cal asked riding alongside the man who huffed for his breath.

"Yes. Yes."

"How?"

"I only wanted to rob them. They went for their guns. It was shoot or die."

Cal scowled at him. "One man was unarmed."

"Hell, it all happened so damn fast—"

"Shorty, hold up. He's going to give us a sworn confession tonight."

When the wagon stopped, Cal motioned for Barton to get up and sit on the back edge of the bed. "You cause me any trouble, you'll run behind this wagon till we get back to Fort Smith."

Barton nodded that he understood and scrambled up on the back of the rig. "Not me boss. Not me boss."

Cal waved for Shorty to go on.

She rode in. "How long have you done this job?"

"Five years."

"Have you ever been shot?"

He scratched his left ear. "Not any that counted."

"What do you mean *counted*?"

"Miss Staunton, you ask more questions than a little kid."

"That's my job."

He reined up his horse and looked hard at her. "Yesiree, you have that hat on backwards."

"Well, I've never worn a hat like this before."

"See that V in the front." He removed his own to show her.

"Yes."

"That serves as a gutter when it rains and forces all the water off your hat way out there."

She turned the hat around as they continued up the dusty road headed for Mud Creek. "I'm learning Marshal Hankins. I really am."

"He lives in those shacks," Chief pointed out to him.

Cal nodded. "Ain't much way in the daylight to sneak up on him is there?"

Chief shook his head. The paint-less, cobbled-up set of small buildings sat on a rise in a large open prairie. Some cooking fire's smoke from a rusty tin pipe rose in the hot winds that swept their faces.

"Miss Staunton, you must stay out here. This could be dangerous. We are leaving the wagon here and going in on horseback to arrest this man."

"Marshal Hankins, I came to get a story. I insist I go with you." She drove her horse up to where Shorty had mounted his horse from behind the wagon. "You can't leave me out here."

In surrender, Cal threw his hands in the air. "I am not responsible for your safety."

"Fine, then let's go."

They spread out, charging across the grassy ground. Each man had his pistol out and urged his horse on. Cal glanced over at her. She looked excited to be in on the chase. He only hoped their actions flushed the whiskey maker out in the open.

A woman and small children rushed outside. Even at the distance, they looked wide eyed and fled the buildings.

"There goes a man," she shouted.

Cal saw him too. "I'll get him." He sent his pony hard after the individual.

A few shots were fired and Cal glanced back. It was only his men giving some warning shots in the air.

He closed the gap and the man stopped, all bent over, coughing and trying to get his breath.

"Joe Highgate?"

"Yes."

"You're under arrest."

The man nodded, still out of wind. "Can I pay a fine here?"

"No, you made too much firewater this time."

Cal dismounted and took two knives off of him. "Get to hiking back."

"Damn, I didn't know what to think—" Highgate shook his head in dismay and started walking. "Four guys came riding me down."

"Three and a reporter from New York."

"He ride like that too?"

"Ain't a he. It's a dad gum old maid. I ain't sure what this world is coming to."

"Neither am I. Tell me what else makes money out here so I don't have to make anymore whiskey."

"Damn it, Highgate. I ain't a social worker or nothing like that." Cal remounted his horse and then he followed his prisoner back to the shacks.

"I know. I know, but there ain't no work around here. Somehow folks find money to buy liquor."

Cal looked up and saw her coming. Oh, now there'd be more questions.

"Is this the man you came to arrest?"

"That's him. But Judge Parker is not liable to hang him."

"I would think not. Sir, could I have your full name?"

"Joe Highgate."

"You've been charged with making spirituous beverages?"

Joe looked up at her. "Whiskey is what they mean."

"Did you know that was against the law to do that in the Indian Territory?"

"No, 'cause I had to eat. There's no work. No crop's worth anything. Pigs are two cents a pound around here and you can't sell 'em."

"And it don't matter about the cost of camels in Africa, it's still illegal to make booze in the Indian Territory," Cal said in disgust.

"That's very profound, Marshal. I may use that in my article, sir."

Dismounting in front of Highgate's main building, Cal saw Joe's short chunky wife and five small kids huddled around her.

"What will we do to eat?" the woman asked. "With him gone?"

"Should have thought about that when he was selling whiskey." She sure didn't look clean enough for him to buy a meal from her for his crew. They'd have to make camp and cook something themselves.

"Where you staying?" the wife asked him.

He knew she'd move down where they parked the wagon and stay close to her man until they went back to Fort Smith. *Camp followers* is what he called them. "Where we setting up at, Chief?"

"Jessup's Store."

"I guess you heard him."

"I did. That's a long ways for me and my young-uns to walk," the woman said, following along with them going back to the wagon.

Don't come then lady—but he kept his peace. Shorty had the prisoner handcuffed and told him to get on the back of the wagon with Barton. Cal finally relented and told her and the kids they could ride in the wagon too.

It was late when they reached Jessup's store. The sun was dipping low in the west and the heat that reflected off the dirt road all day had baked his face. Undoing his latigoes on the saddle girth, he saw how tired Miss Staunton appeared to be doing the same job. A couple more hard days like this one and she'd be ready to go back to Fort Smith.

"Pass out some jerky," Cal said to Shorty. "We've got a big day tomorrow."

His posse man batted his eyes in disbelief at him. Cal frowned away his response so she didn't know that he always made them cook an evening meal.

"If it's any bigger than today," she said, shaking her head, "it will be tough."

"Miss, we can take you back to the Fort Smith road," Cal offered.

"No thank you, sir."

"Very well." She'd be a damn sight harder to discourage than he'd first thought. He'd work on that in the morning.

Shorty found her bedroll and tossed it off the wagon. She drug hers on the ground to the edge of the fire light's circle and began unfurling it. That in place, she went back and asked him for her war-bag. He sprung up in the wagon like his feet were on fire, and handed it down to her. Cal watched her stagger under the weight of the canvas bag. *What did she have in it—rocks?*

The next morning after a breakfast of oatmeal (no sugar or milk) and scalding hot coffee, they saddled their horses. They prepared to leave camp with the prisoners chained to a big oak for all day. The Chief and Shorty were going after an old man charged with pig stealing. Cal planned to arrest a man on Briar Mountain who'd sold an army mule.

"I guess you can go with me today. Hector Bland sold a U.S. army mule. The charge is selling stolen federal property. In that case he must have bought the mule from someone. The prosecutor would like the man's name who delivered it to Bland."

"Do you get hung for stealing mules?" she asked, ready to mount Spook.

"Not in federal court."

When she swung her leg over his back, Spook bogged his head between his knees and took off crow hopping through the prairie grass. Shorty ran out to catch him, but he was no match for the fast bucking horse. The horse kept circling away from him, all the time grunting like a boar hog as he contorted.

When she managed at last to saw his head up and short-loped him in tight circles Cal said, "Well she damn sure rode him."

"Plenty good ride," the Chief said.

"Whew, Miss Staunton, you did right good. He's a bucker ain't he?" Shorty asked.

Out of breath and red faced, she nodded and smiled at their words. "Thanks—he is a handful starting out."

"Now we've got all that over with, let's go find Mr. Bland." Cal gave a head toss and they rode west.

"Is it a long way to his place?" she asked putting her hat back on and drawing up the slide that Shorty had whittled out for her.

"You want to go with them to arrest that pig rustler?"

"No. I merely inquired about what distance we would be going."

"Maybe five or six miles."

"That's fine. I'll put it in my notes. Those two prisoners you chained to the tree this morning will still be there tonight?"

"Yes ma'am. They aren't in as tight a position out here as they will be in Fort Smith federal jail."

She looked squeamish at his mention of that stinking hell hole. Especially in the summer, that jail stunk to high heavens and the Judge's court room above it as well. Whew, he even gave a shudder over the consideration.

"Why are there so many felons out here?"

"It's the last holdout for them. Places in the west are fast getting settled. This land was given to the Indian tribes. They rule over their own people in their own courts, but only Parker's court rules over the whites who Washington never thought would stick around out here when they wrote their treaties."

"It was obviously a large oversight," she said.

"More than that—" He shook his head. The poor woman had no idea the problems caused by the lack of local authority to handle local crimes.

Briar Mountain was a small range of hills covered in post oak. Bland was supposed to have a place on the crest. They followed a deeply washed out wagon road. Steep enough in places that Cal wondered how they ever hauled anything over it.

Then they crossed a bench field that grew blue stem grasses and two horses raised their head. Cal swung off to check them.

"Let me look these ponies over for brands or marks."

Trudy agreed and set Spook down to wait on him. Cal left her holding her reins and resting her hands on the front of that English saddle. The two horses he discovered bore no brands, however their withers were scarred with white hair from saddle sores. *Nothing outstanding about either horse.* Satisfied he rode back to join her.

"Could you tell who owned them?" she asked.

He shook his head. "And they ain't telling either."

The next bench they reached was narrower and at last he spotted a trace of smoke and the cabin on the ridge. "We're about to get there."

She nodded that she heard him.

He took off his hat and mopped his face with his kerchief. "Going to be real hot today."

"Yes, and humid."

A fat, squat-built Indian woman came out of the open front door holding a baby.

"I need to talk to Hector Bland."

"No one here by that name."

"Ma'am, I am a deputy U.S. Marshal. I need to speak to Bland."

"He's not here!"

"Want me to go look in back?" Trudy asked him.

"Yes, but be careful." He stepped off Whiskey. "I figure she's concealing him." He could see the woman's first intention was to block the door and keep him from going inside the house.

"He's too sick," the woman said. Cal moved her and the baby aside to enter the doorway.

"Bland. Where are you?"

"Here. What do you want?"

Cal' s eyes adjusted to the darkness of the cabin's interior well enough that he could see a man in the bed. He also heard the unmistakable metallic click of a handgun being cocked. His boots froze in place. He wanted to run or shoot—neither apparently were options for him at the moment.

Chapter 3

Life and death were the ways of the world west of Fort Smith. Standing frozen in place in the shadowy cabin with a cocked revolver pointed at him made his heart run faster than a steam locomotive. He'd walked right into a trap.

Then Cal heard another voice from outside the open window. "Drop that pistol, mister and raise your hands or you'll be wishing that you had."

"I've got a gun—"

"So have I and I said drop it."

"All right." Bland dropped the revolver on the floor. Striking the floor it went off. He must never have un-cocked it. The room pillowed in acrid gun smoke. Instinctively ducking a speeding shot, Cal dove for the floor, and hit his head on the table leg.

On all fours, he scrambled on the floor for his hat. At that moment, a half crazed large hound in the room that must have been asleep, thought he'd been shot, tore around the room and smashed into Cal. The impact sent him sprawling again on the gritty floor and out of breath. Not recovered from that collision, the woman rushed in to check on her man, tripped and fell right on top of Cal. She knocked the wind out of him and a sharp pain in his side made him wince.

His vision watery from the burning smoke, Cal shouted at the scrambling woman who was stomping and kneeing him to death to escape him. "Get the Sam Hill out of here. You and that dang blame dog both."

"Cal? Cal? Are you all right?"

Who was that calling to him? Miss Staunton. "Yes, yes, thanks to you I am fine, but don't you run in here too. I've been ran over by a dang hound and a fat squaw both."

"You sure you're alright?"

"I'm fine, Miss Staunton." When he went to rise up, he knew better. One of those collisions had broken some of his ribs. The knifing pain ran to his brain.

"Hector Bland you may be dying but you better crawl outside and be quick about it," Cal ordered.

Coughing his head off and barefooted, Bland staggered past Cal who was sitting on his butt holding his side to suppress the pain.

"You sit down right there," his newest deputy ordered, outside the door to the man. "What is her name?"

Still coughing the man managed, "Dorothy."

"Dorothy, bring him some socks and shoes. He will need them where he's going."

Cal by this time was able to rise to his knees, stand with some effort and work his way to the door.

"Are you shot, Marshal Hankins?" Trudy asked blinking her eyes at him.

"No, me and that crazy hound dog that was in here had a train wreck. I think he broke some of my ribs. Then the woman fell right on top of that side and must have broken some more."

"What can I do?"

"Go get some handcuffs out of my saddle bags." He watched her turn to go after them. "By the way, where did you get a gun?"

She turned and grinned at him. "I didn't have one with me. But he didn't know that."

Took a heckuva lot of nerve on her part to do that, he decided. When she returned with the manacles, Bland had on his boots and Miss Staunton told him to put his wrists out and she locked them.

"You got a horse?" Cal asked.

He nodded.

"Tell her to go saddle it for you or you'll have to walk to Jessup's store."

While his woman went to catch Bland's horse, Miss Staunton brought up their mounts. After hitching them in the yard, she came back to speak to Cal. "Which side are they broken on?"

"Right," he said, holding his elbow to his side.

"Must be painful."

"Oh, I'll live."

"They should be bound up, so they will heal."

He frowned at her, "You a doctor too?"

"No, but I've covered enough stories to know about medical practices."

She probably wasn't lying about that. In his discomfort, he couldn't imagine whatever possessed her to challenge that man–unarmed.

At last she had Bland on his horse and a lead rope tied to his mount's halter to lead it. Then Trudy went over to give Cal's butt a shove to get him on board Whiskey. He hit the saddle seeing stars and clutched his side.

To get his attention, she slapped his leg. "You aren't going to fall off on me are you?"

He swallowed hard. "No."

"Good." She mounted hers and taking the lead rope started back.

His vision blurry, Cal clung to the saddle horn with his left hand and took the jarring ride off the mountain. *How would he ever explain how a large hound wrecked him so badly?* He squeezed shut his eyelids but it didn't help the sharp pains going up his side each time Whiskey made a move underneath him.

Hours later, she rode into camp ahead of him and sent Shorty and the Chief over to help him down. *Damn, did she think he was a little kid?* Still he dreaded that step off his horse.

"What did you break?" Shorty asked.

"Some ribs. A damn hound went crazy when a gun that Bland dropped on the floor went off. The dog ran into me doing sixty and knocked me on my ass. Then his squaw came charging in and fell right on top of me." In disgust, he shook his head and eased himself to the ground.

Waving their help away, Cal said, "There's a bottle of toothache medicine in the wagon."

"I'll get some willow bark," the Chief said. "Willow tea will ease your pain."

"How does that work?" she asked him

"Work good. Strong medicine in the bark."

Shorty ran off to get the bottle and the chief went to find some willows. With Bland locked on the chain, Cal followed her to his bedroll holding his right elbow hard to his side.

She offered to help him sit on the ground. He refused her offer and the drop to his knees stabbed him deep in the side. Everything he tried produced the sting of pain. He wanted to be immobilized so nothing did that to him.

The bottle that Shorty handed her read on the label in large letters, "Tooth Ache Medicine." But one whiff of the contents and she laughed. "Real medicine, huh?"

Cal reached for it. "It works on corns, too."

"I'll get you a cup."

"No need. I can drink it out of the neck." Cal simply wanted some quick relief.

What a day. They had gotten their men all right but his broken ribs would slow the operation down.

Squatted beside him, she asked. "Where is the closest doctor?"

"Muskogee I guess, or up at Tahlequah. Why?"

"Well, cracked ribs can puncture your lungs. They can lead to other serious aliments in your body like pneumonia."

"Miss Staunton—"

"My name is Trudy."

"Well, Miss Staunton—"

"No. After today you can start calling me by my given name."

He drew a deep inhale up his nose. "I guess you're right. Anyone can bluff a full grown man that her finger is a pistol, I should accommodate."

"Not accommodate Cal, but out of respect you can call me Trudy."

"Damned if I didn't forget what I was going to argue with you about."

"Good, I think Shorty's stew is ready to eat. Would you like a bowl of it?"

"Yes—ah, Trudy, I sure would appreciate one."

"Stay here. I'll fix it."

"I damn sure ain't running off anywhere."

She looked at the twilight darkening sky for help. "I hope not anyway."

While they ate, seated on the ground, Shorty and Chief had to hear the story over again. They shook their heads laughing how a sleeping hound panicked when the dropped loaded gun went off and then he ran over their boss who was fetching his hat.

The next few days, Cal stayed in camp, supervising the prisoners at chopping more fire wood and food preparation while the other three-some rode off to serve more warrants. Each evening they brought in more prisoners. Cal remained wrought up that he couldn't be doing the same thing and doubling the numbers they received. He wouldn't admit it out loud but he had even begun to endure her company. All day in camp with the grumbling prisoners was not that interesting. The latest five day old newspaper he got from the store each day wasn't his cup of tea to read about some circus elephant stampeding through a crowd during the performance.

On Thursday it rained. Quick thunder showers swept through the camp all day long and he sat on a canvas chair under the large tarp Shorty had stretched overhead for that reason. The prisoners were seated under the wagon—complaining as usual. But he turned a deaf ear to them. *Most useless days of his life.* Too sore to ride a horse and the days were clicking off to Independence Day. For him to have to spend that special holiday out on the Creek Nation prairie would be like—well as boring to him as watching ants work.

"How was your day?" Trudy asked upon their return walking past him in a long tail slicker going for a cup of coffee.

"Boring," his words punctuated by more thunder.

"Want a cup?" she asked

"Sure." Long as he didn't have to get up and get it.

"Oh, it really rained where we were today," she said on her return handing him a fresh cup.

"Have any trouble?"

She shook her head. "These people we've been arresting act very subdued."

"They are. It's the tough ones that can be hard."

"Like Joe Bird was that time we arrested him," Shorty put in.

Cal agreed.

"Who was he?"

"Another felon—made whiskey, stole pigs, horses and robbed people."

"He kill anyone?" she asked, seated cross legged on the small tarp beside Cal's chair

"Yes, in a robbery. He shot the postmaster at Kerry Creek over a seventy-nine cents robbery." A fresh wet wind swept in and struck Cal's face.

"What happened then?" she asked

Cal motioned for Shorty to tell the story.

"Chief tracked him for two days. We found him in camp in the Illinois River breaks. He began shooting at us with a rifle when we rode up this deep canyon. After taking cover in the trees, we exchanged bullets with him for several hours. He was a good shot and man those bullets skipped all around us."

"Did he finally surrender?" she asked

Cal shook his head. "No, he slipped away from us that night, Two days later we got word he was north of us. Go ahead, Shorty."

"A full blood Indian woman told us he was hiding at Heath's. We knew that place. Surrounded it so we were set up for dawn and began our attack. Big Ule Taylor ran out of the house with two guns blazing calling us S-O-B's. We shot him – crazy, damn drunk Indian anyway."

"Two more men crawled out from under Joe Bird's gun-fire, 'for being cowards' Bird said. Once we got them, they told us that Joe was holed up upstairs and had lots of guns and ammo. He also was gobbling like a turkey."

"What's that mean?"

"Cherokee death call," Cal said,

Shorty continued his story. "We planned to burn it down. But about then a Mrs. Redhill came over and begged us not to do that. It was a nice farm house. So Cal with two extra loaded Colts stuck in his belt besides his own, charged the house and finally shot Bird. The man lived to go to trial and Judge Parker hung him."

She whirled and looked hard at Cal. "Were you scared taking on that house and that killer?"

Cal considered his answer. "Some, but that woman was right. It was a fine house."

"That was heroic."

Twisting uncomfortable in the chair at her remark, he shook his head. "No that was dumb, convinced by a nice looking lady to risk my life over torching a good house."

"You're embarrassed over that story." Trudy looked smug about what she had discovered.

"No. It was my job to do it."

"No, I mean the fact that someone complimented you for your bravery."

Cal shook his head. "I think about bravery as the guy who stuck his head up when being shot at and was killed. That's stupidity."

He did feel uncomfortable about his feats. That was why he had Shorty tell the story. It was just a job, just so he made it back for the fireworks was all that bothered him at that moment, still aching every time he moved.

Chapter 4

Seated around the campfire, late that evening, the four of them discussed the remaining warrants they needed to serve. The rain storms had finally passed on eastward and the night air felt much cooler for a change. Listening to the susie bugs sizzling, Cal knew the humidity would be sweltering in the morning.

"Tom—" Cal turned the warrant to the fire light to better read it. "Clark. Resides in the nation near Wiley."

"We can't find a trace of him up here," Shorty said, dismissing with a headshake, any chance to get the man.

"He may have skipped out," Cal said shuffling for the next one. "Carmicoski. Says he's wanted for selling property he did not own."

Trudy asked for the warrant. He handed it over to her. "You know that Pollack?"

After reading it, she handed it back. "No, I was simply curious. The charge is fraud, right?"

Cal agreed with a nod, "Carpenter."

"Joseph Carpenter," Shorty said. "He's a weasel. We've tried to arrest him before and he got away."

"We're down to the hard ones, boys," Cal said. "Howdy Pharr."

"He's a cousin to—" The Chief went to snapping his fingers trying to draw up a name. "Edna Crow."

"Reckon she'd tell us a thing?" Cal asked.

"No, she's sweet on him."

Trudy raised her eyebrows.

Shorty laughed. "Worse things than that go on out here than two cousins living in sin, ma'am."

"Oh. I'm learning."

Tapping his finger on the stack of warrants, Cal said, "We've got four more days to get the rest of these men arrested. I plan on being back to Fort Smith when they set off the fireworks on the Fourth."

His two deputies nodded their heads that they understood his intentions.

The next morning, Shorty saddled Whiskey for him. The gelding acted up some and Cal was about to get upset with him when Trudy rode Spook in close and held onto the bridle for him. He blinked at her actions but thanked her and managed to get in the saddle. He dreaded thinking about this riding business, doing it for a day hurt him but he had no choice.

"We'll ride over to Fort Gibson and see if they know anything about this Carmicoski."

They set out in a trot that jarred him but it was the only way to ever get there. Bright yellow meadow larks, shy pokes and killdeer ran ahead of them after bugs. Bob white quail flushed a time or two at their approach on the wagon road. The day's temperature was still cool but the rising sun would soon heat it to scorching levels by mid afternoon.

"Folks aren't run away friendly toward you lawmen are they?" she asked riding beside him.

He nodded his head, holding inside much of the pain he felt. "Naw—Marshals mean we're here to arrest someone. It may be a brother, cousin or friend."

"It also is dangerous."

His own laughter stabbed him, "Yeah, getting run over by a crazy hound."

"That man would have shot you."

"Yes, you saved my life and I am beholding."

She looked at the sky for help. "I didn't do that—I—I simply helped you."

"Now who's acting shy about doing something?"

"Maybe, but you do much braver things than that. I heard those two talk about your other feats."

He brought Whiskey down to a walk that felt better. "This law business is not easy."

"I was wondering. Is there anyplace out here to take a bath?"

He'd not thought about it, wasn't spring time. *A place for her to take a bath. Maybe over in the Grand River—would she want to do that?* Dang, taking a bath was not high on his list of things to do at that moment.

"I reckon you could bathe in the river when we get over there. We can find a private place for you to do that."

She nodded. "That would be nice. Sponge baths are really not the same."

He agreed and kicked Whiskey into a trot. At this rate they'd never get there.

Past noon they arrived at the square fort built of logs. The stores and shops filled several building that faced the inside parade grounds. No troopers were there any longer. Several blanket-wrapped Indians loafed around the place. A few near-naked red skinned children played in mud holes.

He dismounted gingerly, said he'd only be a minute or two and went in under the porch the entire fort shared over the walk. The door bell jingled over head when he opened the door to Schilling's store. The smiling face of Martha Schilling met him.

"Marshal Hankins what can I do for you?"

"I need a fine bar of soap. Not lye. And two towels."

"I have some sweet smelling soap that is supposed to be very good."

"You ever use it?"

"It costs twenty-five cents a bar," she said in a shocked whisper. "I couldn't afford to use it."

He agreed that was a very high priced commodity. "I'll take it and two towels."

She brought him the best towels too, called them Turkish. He paid her the dollar and thanked her. He was about to leave when he recalled the real reason why he rode over there.

"You know of a man named Carmicoski?"

"What do you need from him?"

"I have a warrant for his arrest for fraud."

"He stays with the Hutchison family. They live west and north of here if that is your man."

"I bet there ain't many by that name in the territory."

Martha smiled politely at him. "No, I don't think there is."

He went back outside and put his purchases in the saddle bags. "We may be lucky. Think I may have found him."

She nodded, "He around here?"

"After you get that bath, we'll go and see about him."

Her face turned red. "You don't have to—"

"That's what you wanted. The river is right over there."

She chewed on her lower lip. "Will it be private?"

"I think we can find such a place."

"Well—"

"Come on girl. It's bath time."

She looked around the square. A blacksmith was beating on something making it ring like a bell. A man was cussing a team of mules that wouldn't "get over" for him. Several women under bonnets were crossing the yard.

"No bathhouses here?"

"Nope, none."

"Then," she said as if gathering her courage. "The river will have to do."

He agreed and mounted up.

They soon found a place under the cottonwood and sycamores trees where a shoal made a beach. She hobbled the horses to let them graze on the flat above it. He fetched the towels and soap out of his saddle bags and placed them in her hands.

"You bought them for me?"

He looked around. "Ain't no one else here is there?"

"Oh, what wonderful smelling soap."

"Thought you'd like it, now you go take a bath and I'll keep a look out up here."

"It's not very private." she said, sounding like she had second thoughts about it.

"Only God, some crows and maybe a hawk are going to see you. It won't shock them."

She began to laugh and shake her head. "What could they see anyway?"

With that she leaned over, kissed him then with her bathing things in her hands went down the slope. He was still tasting his lips where her mouth touched his.

Now why did she go do that? He pulled up a pinch of grass and threw it in the growing wind. Why? What had come over him to stop and buy her some expensive soap and two towels—Turkish towels at that. Why Mrs. Schilling probably hadn't sold any of them in months. Flour sacks would do most folks to dry with anyway if they did fall in the river.

"Marshal?"

Was she calling him?

"Marshal Hankins?"

He went over to the edge of the bank. Why she was neck deep in water, dog paddling in the river.

"The water is wonderful. You should try it."

Now? She meant for him to join her. As a boy in Texas he'd skinny dipped with a neighbor girl named Jubalee. That had been risky. If her paw ever found out he'd horse whipped him. But she was kinda of wild anyway compared to the rest of the teenage girls he knew back then. And she got him in the water on a dare, the first time anyway.

Then he watched Trudy swim away. He went ambling off the bank and soon was on the shoal beach.

"I won't look," she said in water up to her neck with her back to him.

"Good," he said turned away from her to undress and feeling as hot faced as a man could get.

When at last the hot wind swept his bare skin, he turned and saw she still remained facing away. Good. The gravel was sharp on his soles and he soon was out in the warm water and waist deep.

"I'm here," he said.

"Doesn't it feel good?"

"I haven't really thought about it—yet."

Like a river otter she dove off and swam away from him. Her freckled skin looked sleek. He forgot about time. He forgot about why he was there. It was the river's current sweeping past him, the too bright sun sparkling on the water and her that filled his every thought. It wasn't that way in Texas swimming with Jubalee—he worried the whole time her father would show up and kill him.

He soon joined Trudy and they swam together across the river and back. *Why couldn't he take his eyes off of her?* He wasn't trying to see her naked body parts. It was her dancing green eyes and the shape of her mouth that hypnotized him. The wet short hair plastered to her skull, laughing freely, she waded over to him and he held her in his arms.

His eyes closed against the sun, he savored the tender moment and his precious gift.

"We better get dressed," she said bringing him back to reality.

"Yes," he said and turned to wade out of the water.

"Why did your parents name you California?"

"My mother wanted to go there when I was born."

"Did she ever go there?"

He shook his head. "She lived and died in Texas."

"Here, use one of these towels to dry with." She shoved it at him.

"Hot as it is. You'll dry fast." He used it and soon had his shirt on and then his pants. Dressed he felt much more comfortable,

"That ease your pain any?" she asked, tying on her riding skirt at the waist.

"Some." He'd been so busy simply being with her, he'd almost forgotten the discomfort of it all.

"I feel wonderful," she said and caught his hand going up the bank. He squeezed it to show her he was there. It had been almost twenty years since he'd held a woman's hand walking with her. Zypta Monahan. He'd come home from the war on leave. She was two years older than he was. They were even going to be married when the war was over and he came home for good. But she couldn't wait that long and instead two months later married Phil Stephens when he came home on leave.

Pulling Trudy up on the high bank with his good arm, he found her up against his chest–one of those moments when a man wasn't sure what he should do—fearful she'd get angry if he kissed her. *What the hell?* He kissed her anyway.

It turned out to be a long one. When they were through he checked the sun time. Mid afternoon. *How long had they swam?* No telling. He'd lost track of time. He dug some jerky out of his saddlebag sand handed some to her.

"We better eat. Then go see if we can find that guy."

"Whatever you say Cal."

She'd never called him that before either. His side was feeling less painful or he hadn't noticed. *This—this—what would he call it?* No words in his mind for it but he'd damn sure lost his mind in that river. An Injun would say something cast a spell over him. Spell or not they better find this Pollack and get back to camp.

He stopped at a cross road store and asked about the Hutchison's farm. The man came outside like he wanted his directions right and used his flat hand to describe the way to their place. Cal thanked him and then mounted up and they rode north a mile and went west on the section line road.

A batch of curs ran out to bark at them. Cal hissed them away. The place looked trashy and the low roofed soddy was not well built.

A man came outside, putting up his overall straps and looked fish eyed at the two of them. "Whatcha need?"

"Mr. Carmicoski."

"Ain't no one here by that name, my name's—"

"Your name's Hutchison. Mine's Hankins. I'm a U.S. Marshal and I have a warrant for this man."

"He ain't here."
"When will he be back?"
"Didn't say."
"You know harboring a criminal is a serious offense?"
"Wasn't harboring him. He just came by and stayed a few days."
"That's harboring him."

Hutchison shrugged. He looked up when his woman came to the door. "He done told yah he ain't cheer."

His missus had lost her upper front teeth and she wore a dress that had been washed to death. It fit her better before she'd gained some weight too. Her oily stringy hair hadn't been brushed since Noah had his ark and she squeaked when she said, "He ain't *cheer.*"

"I heard you but I may need to look around."
"Look all you want, I said he—"
"He ain't here," Cal said. "I heard you." He handed his reins to Trudy.

"What's he done anyway?"
"Sold a farm he didn't own." Cal went around the soddy, shooing dogs and scattering hens dusting in the shade. If he was hiding it might be in the root cellar. He drew his six gun and then careful like drew open the door.

"Come on out!" he ordered.

The sight of the face of the man with his hands raised stopped his heart for a moment. Well, he'd be a dead fish. He'd found his man by pure damn luck.

"Get out here. You must be Carmicoski. I'm a U.S. Marshal and I have a warrant for your arrest."

"I figured that you did. I just didn't get out of the country soon enough, did I?"

"I guess not."

The man walking ahead of him looked to be in his thirties. No weapon on him. Hardly like the hardened criminals that he usually rounded up, nor like the dumb ones. This man could have been a business man, but that's how a flimflam man looked—innocent.

"That him?" Trudy asked.

"It's him all right." Cal scowled at the man who owned the place. "Hutchison I ought to take you in for harboring him."

"Aw, don't do that Marshal, please," the missus pleaded.

"Go get him a horse to ride. He has one, don't he?"

Hutchison agreed and took off to get it.

Cal handcuffed his prisoner and told him to sit there on a crate. It took Hutchison a long time to saddle the man's horse and bring him up. When he finally came with the horse, Cal put a lead on it and she rode in to take the rope.

He helped Carmicoski into the saddle and they headed back without hardly another word spoken between the two. They were long hours away from their base camp and the sun was setting in the west. After a long look at the red flare in the western sky, he rode up and clapped his hand on her shoulder.

"It was a good day, Trudy."

She swallowed hard and nodded. "I don't regret a thing."

With a nod he agreed. Wasn't anything to regret about this day. Two grown people had a damn nice experience that would be hard to forget. She'd go back to New York one day and he'd sure miss her. They'd better trot or they'd never get back.

Way into the night riding into camp they awoke Shorty. He lit a candle lamp and carried it around locking the prisoner on the chain and then came back to hold the light up for them to unsaddle by.

"You found him," Shorty said. "And we got the weasel this time, too."

"Wonderful. We can head in day after tomorrow."

"Why then?"

"Because I'm going to sleep that long."

Shorty laughed.

Saddles piled on the ground, Cal took his horse and the prisoner's out to be hobbled in the meadow. "She and I don't need a light, Shorty. There are enough stars out. Go back to bed. We're going that way too."

He put the hobbles on both horses then went over to help her. That done, he threw his good arm over her shoulder, "Guess you've got enough story today?"

She clutched his hand on her shoulder and slowly shook her head. "I'm not going to write that up. But I won't forget it."

"Neither will I." Then they parted and went to their own bedrolls.

When he was seated on his roll and pulling off his boots he regretted not kissing her again. *Should have done that.* Oh well, he better get some sleep.

The sun blinded him when he finally stirred awake the next morning. *Must have slept till noon.* He pulled on his pants under the covers and got up to put on his shirt. There was some kind of argument going on about the prisoners. His socks on, he fought his boots. Them in place, he went strapping his side arm around his waist going toward the argument, he wondered what was wrong?

Shorty was arguing with that fat squaw that had fallen on him. He waded in between them.

"What's this all about?"

"You are going to let him die?" she said, pointing at her peaked looking man seated on the ground.

"Hey, we didn't get him in this fix. We're going to Fort Smith in the morning."

"He will die."

"What should we do?" Cal finally asked her.

"I will take him home and make him well."

"I can't do that. You will have to make him well here."

She stomped off swearing in English about those damned marshals. Cal shook his head at Shorty. "You can't make them all happy."

Shorty agreed. Trudy joined them. Her face looked freshly washed and her hair was brushed in place. Under the Stetson, she still looked sleepy. "What was wrong?"

"A woman wanted us to release her man."

"I would want my man released too."

"We've got company coming." Cal squinted against the glare. "It sure looks like Marshal Johnson and some other marshals."

"You're right," Shorty said. "Must be important or he'd not be out here."

Cal walked down to greet his boss.

Hal Johnson looked over things and swung down. "I need to talk to you Hankins—privately."

With a nod for the men that had rode in with Johnson, Cal walked off to the side with his boss, "Sounds serious."

"It is serious. The Davis Brothers held up the Katy train near Vinita and took $80,000 dollars from the express car."

"How long ago?"

"They have a two day head start on you right now. I'm already catching all kinds of hell from Washington about this. I want you and your posse men to go up there and find them."

"Who else did you send up here?"

"Dummies. They found nothing."

"Maybe there isn't anything to find."

"No, there were over a half dozen or more men held up that train. They had fresh horses and they had to eat and they had to—"

"What about my prisoners?" Cal asked.

"We'll take them back for you and you'll get full credit for everything."

Cal nodded then made a pained face at his boss. "Six arrests is only twelve dollars. Hardly worth my time to go up there."

"I'll sign you up as a special deputy. Three dollars a day and you can collect the railroad and express company reward for ten thousand dollars."

"Pay my men two dollars a day?"

Johnson never hesitated. "I'll handle it. When can you leave here?"

"Traveling light, we can go in an hour. Of course we'll have meal expenses without the wagon."

"Covered, stay in hotels. I'll pay for them."

"We'll get ready to go then." *Dang*. There went his chances to be in Fort Smith for the Fourth Celebration. "I want a description of the robbers. I don't want to ride by them."

"I have one with me. What we have on them. Hankins, I'm counting on you."

"Far as we are behind them, it may be a fool's deal. I'll talk it over with my men."

"Good." Johnson removed his silk rimmed Stetson hat at her approach. "How are you today Miss Staunton?"

"Fine, sir."

"He and the marshals with him are taking our prisoners into Fort Smith for us." Cal said. "They've had a major train robbery up at Vinita two days ago by the Davis gang and Marshal Johnson wants us to find them."

"Who are they?" she asked Johnson.

"Two brothers who've been in and out of trouble since the war. They probably rode with Quantrill during the war like the James brothers did. This is their first big heist and they really must have had inside information on this shipment."

"Pinkerton men are crawling like ants all over the place up there, aren't they?" Cal asked.

Johnson nodded.

"I better tell the Chief and Shorty. Miss Staunton if you're going along load your bedroll—no, we'll figure out a pack horse to haul them." Realizing her saddle had no place for it. "But we'll have to travel light."

"I understand," she said quietly.

"You're going with them?" Johnson asked her.

"Of course, I want the story of this gang's arrest."

The Chief Marshal looked horrified. "It may be dangerous."

"It's been that up here." She laughed out loud at his obvious concern.

"Shorty," Cal said and with a head toss that got the attention of his man.

"What's wrong?" The short man waded over looking concerned. "We'll have to have more food if we feed all them too." He indicated the new arrivals with Johnson.

"They can cook for themselves," Cal said. "We need to load our bedrolls and war-bags on two pack horses. There's been a big train robbery up at Vinita. Marshal Johnson wants us up there to investigate. Miss Staunton's going too."

Shorty's blue eyes narrowed at the news. "Right now, huh?"

"Yeah, he's taking our wagon and prisoners in for us."

"Man, this must be serious."

"It is."

"Who did it?"

"The Davis brothers."

Shorty made a face and looked to be considering them. "I've heard they were tough."

Cal agreed. "No one's found a trace of them in two days."

"I'll round up some pack saddles. Guess we can buy some of the prisoners' horses to use, if he'll buy them."

"I'll check on that."

Looking serious, Shorty dropped his head and shook it. "There goes your celebration."

"Ah, there will always be another." Cal clapped him on the shoulder.

"You and her better eat something," Shorty said, "before they find it. I've saved you some."

Things went to moving. Johnson put a marshal called Yancey in charge of getting things ready for them to start back with the prisoners for Fort Smith. Cal and Trudy had a plate of beans, and biscuits while everyone rushed around.

"Keep up with all my things," Cal told the new man stopping him for a second. "I paid for that wagon, team, pots, pans and not the court."

"We will. We will." And he was off to see about something else.

Cal could see by comparison to how his men did all that so smoothly that he'd hardly noticed it. Chief nodded over his coffee cup about all their flittering around to get ready to leave. "Good to have lots of them to do my job."

"Right. We need to be on the road shortly."

"Shorty told me."

"You know these men we're going after?"

"I have been around where they were."

"Good, see one, signal me."

Chief agreed.

In record time, they had three pack horses loaded. Cal winced at that large a pack train but he couldn't see leaving any of her things behind. Besides, Johnson paid for the horses and packsaddles with script so it never cost him anything. He shook hands with his boss, ready to leave.

"Hankins, you find them. I don't care about the cost."

"If they're out there. We'll find them."

"I know. That's why I came to get you for the job. Send me wires about any progress whenever you can."

"I will."

Chapter 5

July 3, 1882 – Vinita, Indian Territory

To: Chief Marshal Hal Johnson U S Federal Courthouse Fort Smith Arkansas

Have located a track stop obvious collusion in this crime stop headed after them stop inform top Pinkerton officials I will tolerate no more interference stop

U S Deputy Marshal California Hankins

Cal stood on the board walk outside the telegraph office for a brief moment and studied the building clouds. It would rain that afternoon. He nodded to the three riders. "I sent him the information."

He took the reins from her, and mounted. He nodded at Shorty. "Told him I wanted no more Pinkerton men interfering in our business."

"Good."

They crossed the tracks and headed down the dusty dirt street of false fronted stores and pool halls. No bars or saloons, of course—the Indian Territory was dry. They soon were out on the rolling prairie headed west. Chief had word that someone out in the Cherokee Strip might be hiding the gang. This land was mostly leased by cattlemen who operated out of Kansas. There was an outfit on the South Fork of the Arkansas—the K T L outfit where Homer Davis was the superintendent.

K T L leases lay on west of the Osage Reservation. A country neither Cal nor his crew was familiar with. But the Chief found out enough from an Osage buck he had librated with wildcat whiskey to learn about Homer Davis and his kinship to the notorious brothers.

Shorty learned from some Texas hands that some of the men who hung around town were suspected to be in on the robbery. They rode H T branded horses. Trudy, by telegram (Cal felt Pinkerton wouldn't check on her wires like they did all of his), said that the H T brand was also registered to the K T L company. Things had gone fine until several Pinkerton men had jumped them with rifles at the Millhouse Livery.

"What's your part in this?" a fat man in a fancy suit asked while his men disarmed them.

"What's your name?" Cal demanded.

"Rupart Cline. I am—"

"You're bullshit. We're U.S. Deputy Marshals and you are interfering in our business. That's a federal offense. Now hand back our guns or you're going to do time."

"I want to know why you're snooping in our business."

"I don't have to explain a damn thing to you. You all have had a week to solve this crime and have done nothing. Now, our weapons or I'm filing charges." Cal was pointing his finger like a pistol at the man.

"Give them their guns back," Cline surrendered.

"Once more. Stay out of my way." Cal slapped his Colt in his holster. "Come on," he said to his crew. "We're going to supper."

Trudy laughed all the way to the café that evening. "You know we read all the time about the wonderful Pinkerton Agency stopping crime and capturing criminals. This bunch here are really some bloated egotists."

"That a disease?" Shorty asked. "Ego-whatever?"

"No, it means all swelled up about their self importance," she said.

Shorty agreed. "That suits 'em."

The waiter in the hotel restaurant looked hard at the Chief while waiting to take their order.

"He won't kill anyone," Call said off handed to draw the man's attention away. "If he does he won't eat them. I want the roast beef."

"Oh, yes, sir."

Amused, Trudy shook her head when the four of them were at last alone seated at the table. "Has that man never seen an Indian in here?"

"I guess not." Cal lowered his voice. "I'll wire Hal in the morning and we can leave."

"Will Pinkerton follow us?" Shorty asked.

"Probably."

Chief nodded. "Plenty country out there to lose them in."

They all laughed.

***

Leaving Vinita mid morning, as obvious as they could be, they headed west. Cal felt he'd thrown the gauntlet down at

Cline. He'd better not mess with a U.S. Marshal. He'd show him some teeth. If he didn't believe that telegram he'd sent his boss—he felt certain that Cline had access to that message and any others they sent. Maybe Trudy's had slipped past him about the brand source, besides Cline had no idea about that ranch. Without the Chief's Osage knowledge and Shorty's efforts to loosen up some cowboys with a pint or two of shine, he'd not known anything either.

Two days of hard riding ahead to reach the Salt Fork country. If the gang was there, it would be pure luck but they might learn more. Only lead they had. The K T L cow camp.

"Who do you think tipped them off about the money shipment?" Trudy asked.

"I figure they paid someone well for that information. I warned Hal there was collusion in that deal. Let him look into it."

"I see. This Homer Davis is a cousin of theirs?" she asked.

"Some kin anyway. Blood's thicker than water in this case I figure. They needed a good isolated place to cool their heels. This ranch would be the place."

"And they used ranch horses."

"Who would know them? H T brand meant nothing to those Pinkerton men if they saw it. They damn sure weren't cowboys. Shorty's new Texas cowhand buddies never let a horse go by they didn't note his brand."

"What will they do with that all that money?" she asked.

"Probably spend it in a cat house in Wichita."

"Eighty-thousand dollars?" She looked about to strangle.

"They wouldn't be the first ones. If we don't trot these horses we'll never find out."

Deep in the Osage Nation, they found an Indian woman cooking "stew." Cal sent Trudy over to smell and taste it. It wasn't unusual to find such "open air" food places at cross roads tended by Indian women. A dime would buy you a meal.

"It smells all right," Trudy said returning. "We need our cups to get some. Her dishes don't look clean enough."

"Fine," Shorty said untying his from the saddle tie.

Chief brought a turtle shell. Cal and Trudy had their tin cups too. They feasted on their meal with the wrinkled faced old woman shuffling around refilling their utensils with a gourd dipper.

Cal paid her two quarters and refused any change. They rode on after supper to make camp by a small stream. A short ways out of their camp, he stood guard while she took a bath and washed her clothing. Letting her clothes dry on some bushes, she wore a house dress and came to sit by him in the twilight.

"You know one day you'll be too old to do this job."

"Maybe an outlaw's bullet will retire me for good before then."

"Retire you?"

"Yes, I mean put me across the great divide."

"That sounds suicidal. I don't think you are that big of a coward, Cal Hankins."

He hugged his knees. "What are you getting at?"

"Well—if you did get that reward for capturing these men, you might buy a place of your own."

"I might."

"You don't sound interested."

"Lord, woman, I've been on my own since I was thirteen. Had the sugar foot all these years, you think I could stay home and tend chickens?"

"I don't know what you can do and can't do. I'm just thinking you aren't getting any younger."

He laughed. "That's for sure. Why haven't you ever married and settled down?"

"I was supposed to marry a man—once."

"Once, huh?"

"He was killed in the war. Gettysburg."

"Sorry."

"No, I haven't talked much about it. But I always felt the war cheated me."

"It cheated lots of us." *Too many of us.*

"My clothes will dry by morning. We better go and get some sleep." She rose and pulled him to his feet. "Hold me for a minute. It's lonely out here listening to owls hoot and those coyotes who you claim are not wolves howling."

To have her in his arms, did more than stir up his manhood, it gave him a new power. Something he'd never felt before. *Maybe he could tend chickens if he had a woman like her—and be satisfied. No telling.* He smelled her fresh hair. These were nice moments in his life. Even if nothing came of them, he could relive them over and over again. Those times that he shared with her.

***

At dawn they rode away. They crossed into the badlands. Red rock outcroppings and small mesas, a barren land, little inhabited and hardly like the tall grass country behind them. The chalky alkali rims left where creeks and water holes had evaporated made Cal's tongue want to withdraw. Then they were out of the badlands and back into waving grassland that rolled away from them. The third day they reached the Salt Fork of the Arkansas.

They stopped and bought food from a woman named Lenore Kimes who lived in a dugout. A young woman as glad to see them as they were to find her. They had coffee but she'd been out of the good stuff for a month. Her husband was a line rider for the cattlemen's organization that rented part of the Strip. His job was ride and turn back strays if they tried to leave the Strip. "He only comes back in every three days, stays at home a day then he rides the other direction for three more," Lenore explained.

"Do you get lonely out here, Lenore?" Trudy asked her.

"Sure, but I read the Bible and sew. Keeps my mind occupied."

"You're brave young woman," Trudy said.

Cal agreed as he sipped on the first good coffee they'd had time for in three days. *She must really love her man to put up with this dark hole and being by herself for days.*

"I do some gardening. The boss man brought me enough wire to fence off a garden plot. I have some beans, squash, some corn and tomatoes."

She fixed them rice, gravy, and biscuits. Her food drew the saliva in Cal's mouth. Seated on the ground eating their meal, and swept by the strong south wind, he asked her about the K T L outfit.

She looked hard at him. "You are lawmen right?"

"Yes, we are."

"All right. My husband says too many drifters go in and out of that place. I think he's a good judge of people. They must be ten miles up stream from here. His boss told him that by himself he was not to try to stop any rustlers. But I fear he would. He rides for the brand."

"You think they're rustlers?" Trudy asked.

"I ain't proof positive. They mostly avoid me and I'm glad but several nights bawling cattle have woken me up." She looked them over for their impression.

"We're here looking for outlaws," Cal said. "Really train robbers."

"I can't help you, but you ride north and stay close to the Salt Fork you'll find their outfit up there."

"Thanks, Lenore for all you have done for us. This food was wonderful. The government will pay you."

"Taking money for feeding hungry people would be wrong. Marshal, I will pray for you and your people's safety."

"Thank you," he said.

"And for breakfast we'll have pancakes. I have some lick left."

Her words drew smiles from the other men. Cal was worried they'd eat her out of food. "We don't want to run you out—"

"No problem, sir. It was my own fault. My coffee order was just way too short."

That evening under the stars, Cal and Trudy walked the high bank above the bottomland sliced by the silver meandering Salt Fork. Her hand closed in his swung between them to the crickets' chorus.

"Your side is better?" she asked.

"Much better. Oh, it's still tender, but I'm fine."

"Good. You know she is such a brave girl. Staying out here, alone, and not losing her mind. He's a lucky guy to have her."

"Life in the west is like this."

"I'm going to write a story about her. People back east need to know about women like Lenore."

He stopped and gathered her in his arms. "Did I ever say how much I enjoyed your company? I'm not run over with fancy words and they come hard. You have a life and I have a life and our paths crossed west of Fort Smith. Two travelers—alone in this world. Self sufficient by themselves and yet we cling to each other."

"Like we've known each other for ages?"

"Yes. Kinda like my boots. Worn to fit my feet and maybe I don't appreciate them enough."

"There's a cold reality to all this. This is your life." She chewed on her lower lip before she went on. "Mine's over a thousand miles from here."

"I know. But did you ever eat a real good ripe watermelon?"

"Yes, I have."

"Man oh man, it was good. The best you ever had. I guess we're having one of those special county fair winning watermelons."

"And when it's gone we can remember it?"

"Yes." And he kissed her.

Chapter 6

Mid day they found the K T L outfit as Lenore had told them they would. Cal used his army binoculars to study the place. They had a grizzly faced cook in a once white apron. There was an Indian boy down there, splitting shovel wood from the pile. Some drovers were watching a cowboy breaking a horse in the corrals.

"How many are there?" Shorty asked bellying down beside him in the grass.

"A half dozen I can see not counting the cook and Indian boy."

"Chief, you've seen the Davis Brothers. Look that place over down there and tell me if you see the Davis brothers."

Chief crawled up beside him, took the glasses and studied them for long while. Then he shook his head. "None of them are the Davis brothers."

"Shit!" He'd been afraid of that. They'd rode out here hoping—

"You know a cowboy we arrested one time at McAlister named O'Neal?" Chief asked.

Cal closed his eyes. "O'Neal? O'Neal? What did they want him for?"

"I recall the name," Shorty said making another scope of the place. "But not why he was arrested."

"He's down there. What we going to do?" Chief asked.

"We came a long ways." On his hands and knees, he moved backwards until it was safe to stand and no one could see him. He went over the hill to where she held the horses.

"See them?" she asked.

"Chief says the two brothers aren't down there."

"Oh, now what do we do?"

"We're going to ride down there and tell them who we are and we have a search warrant."

"You do?"

"Oh, yes. All I have to do is fill it out." He fetched it out of the saddle bag and using a pencil put in the K T L operations in the Cherokee Strip. Completed, he slipped it in the inside pocket of his vest. "Everyone get their rifle out. I don't want anyone shot. But I sure don't want any of us shot either."

A grim nod and they all mounted up. "Trudy, you stay back with the pack horses. If hell breaks loose, you ride for it."

"I can shoot a gun."

"I know but you worry about our pack horses."

"Yes, sir."

Cal led the way. Whiskey with his wind swept tail must have felt the tension so he single footed toward the corrals and sod buildings. Even at the distance, Cal could see them discovering the posse's approach and pointing in their direction. Someone ran to the low roof main building and soon a big man came out to look at them.

"He's a Davis," the Chief said from behind Cal.

"I figure he must be the foreman."

"Yeah."

"Spread out," Cal told his two.

"That's close enough," the big man said, facing them off.

"You Homer Davis?" Cal asked, making certain his men were taking places at least thirty feet apart from him."

"Who're you?"

"U.S. Deputy Marshal Cal Hankins of Fort Smith. These men are my deputies."

Davis folded his arms over his chest. "You're Parker's men, huh?"

"That's right. I suggest you all drop your firearms on the ground and stand back from them."

"You must be here on business?"

"Davis, I gave you and your men an order. Now, real easy lift that six-gun out with two fingers, drop it and step back."

"There's more of us than you."

"You keep thinking like that. Your men may get us but you won't be alive to notice."

"Drop your guns men."

The strained long moment passed. They dropped their guns and backed away from them. Shorty stepped down and covering them with his rifle, he moved the seven men to stand at the corral fence.

"Call your cook and that Indian boy out here too."

"Zinc, come on out. Bring that kid too."

Drying his hand on his apron and squinting out of one good eye, the bushy faced cook and the slip of a boy came outside. Shorty motioned them to join the others.

"What is it you want?" Davis asked.

"I want to know which one of your men helped your cousins rob the Katy mail car."

"My men been here—"

"Davis, I have several eye witnesses that will testify that K T L horses were in Vinita at the time of the robbery."

"What robbery?"

"It happened a week ago. And they might even recognize some of this crew as loafing around the town. Which four of you was it?" Cal looked over the men looking hang dog and not replying to his request.

"Not me," a bowlegged puncher said.

"Shut up Farrel," Davis said, cutting around to stare him down.

"No," Cal said. "Farrel keep talking. Come out here. Who was in Vinita last week?"

"I'll check the house," Trudy said dismounting and hitched her string of horses to a rail.

"You ain't got any authority—"

"Oh, I have a search warrant signed by Judge Isaac Parker to check these premises out. Go ahead Trudy."

"You won't find anything." Davis sullied.

"Anyone else didn't go to Vinita last week?"

Another puncher raised his hand and came forth to stand with Farrel.

"You made a mistake and even a bigger one coming here. There were no K T L horses in Vinita last week." Davis sounded sure of himself.

"How about an H T brand on the right shoulder–that's the company's horse brand, isn't it?"

"Cal, you might want to see this," she called to him from the doorway.

Cal stopped and looked hard at Davis. "That is the company's horse brand, isn't it Davis?"

For a moment longer Cal hesitated and then Davis nodded. Satisfied he had the man dead to rights, Cal hurried over to the house. Forced to duck to enter, he straightened inside. She held out a canvas bag to him. He turned it to the light to read the label.

St. Louis Federal Reserve Bank.

"Darling, you just found the spoiler in the entire deal." Rapping the back of his fingers on the sack, he laughed. He really had part of the gang outside. *Where was the loot?*

He kissed her on the cheek and ducked the lintel going outside. "Let's start cuffing the rest of them. Farrel and you come over here."

"He's Grover," Farrel said. "I swear we ain't had no part and ain't got none of that blood money."

Grover was shaking. "He—he –ain't lying mister. I knew it. I knew the law would come get them. I've been scared enough since they got back to pee in my pants."

"Where's the Davis Brothers?"

Farrel swallowed hard. "Medicine Lodge."

"How long since they were here?"

"Two-three days?" Farrel looked over at Grover for assurance.

Grover nodded but he wouldn't look up at Cal. "I knowed the law'd get 'em. I just knew."

Cal thanked them then he shouted to the cook. "Zinc, you and that boy better fix us a meal. We're all hungry."

"K T L will hire a lawyer and have us out of jail in a day," Davis said from his seat on the ground. "They have plenty of power in Washington D.C. You'll lose your badge for taking us in. You'd better think about it."

"If all you've got to do out here is rob trains, they may not need you either."

Cal herded Zinc in the main house and the old man grumbled. "How in hell's name did you ever find 'em."

"Ask that Injun out there. He's our tracker."

Trudy laughed out loud. Then she covered her mouth with her hands as if embarrassed. She shook her head and went outside.

"I guess you know this is serious business," Cal said to the cook.

"Mister, all I do is cook here. I don't ask nothing. Don't know nothing."

"Do you know where those brothers went up there?"

"Medicine Lodge. I heard them guys tell you."

"Where?"

"You mean what cat house they went to?"

"I'm asking."

Zinc shook his head. "Marlene's probably."

"Which end of town is it in?"

"West end. It's a rambling one story soddy that's been added on to several times. You can't miss it. She flies some bloomers on a flag pole out front." Zinc chuckled.

"Thanks. I'll leave my men in charge. Feed the prisoners and them. No tricks. I promise you I'll leave you, the boy and them other two behind when I take those others in later."

Zinc nodded that he understood. "I damn sure never got a penny of it."

"I believe that. Better get them some food."

He agreed.

Cal went outside and she joined him. "Sorry I laughed about your statement."

"Why? It was funny."

She shook her head. "No, this whole thing has been serious. I see now very well why Marshal Johnson sent you."

Cal shrugged. "Any good lawman could have figured it out. Pinkerton didn't."

"You said any good—you don't like them do you?"

"They're all right. They don't have the man power I have. Shorty knows those cowboys. He learned about the horse brands. Chief learned about the other parts. I have a good working team." Cal laughed. "All of us misfits, but it works."

"What now?"

"I need to ride in and arrest those two before they get the sugar foot and leave out."

Trudy raised an eye brow. "You know where they are?"

"Zinc told me Marlene's."

"What is that?"

"A house of ill repute."

"I'll go with you."

"It ain't a place for you."

She scowled at him. "I'm not going to work there."

He felt his face redden. "I never meant that."

"Good. I can pack a gun. I can shoot one. You may need some help."

He agreed with a small nod. That many prisoners out here–he better leave both of his men to guard them. If he took the prisoners into that town, it might tip his hand. He wanted those two brothers. For years they'd proven themselves elusive.

"After we get something to eat, we'll head up there."

"Is there any money inside?" Shorty asked when he and the Chief squatted on the ground for a pow-wow with Cal.

"There could be some," Cal said to his deputies. "You can look and quiz them. We're going to keep them prisoners here until I can locate the two Davis brothers. You two can stay here and watch them. Maybe you can learn from Homer where his share of the money is at." Cal looked over at the dejected prisoners then back to his two men. "They may try an escape. They'll need close watching."

"We can do all that while you're gone. You be careful. Those two are tough hombres," Shorty said.

"I will. Trudy and I are leaving after whatever meal this is coming up."

Shorty grinned. "I'm ready for food, whatever you call it. Guess she knows these are real tough outlaws—the brothers."

"I've warned her, like talking to a fence post."

"Pretty good one," Chief said, "for a white woman."

Cal glanced over where she waited for him with her butt against a hitch rack, and chewing on a grass stem. "Yes, she is."

Zinc's food tasted fresh. The K T L boys ate well, he could tell, though when or if they ever did any work, he wasn't certain. Handcuffed, they soon learned how to eat. Shorty had them each locked on a long chain. It prevented any running off.

In late afternoon, Cal and Trudy headed north on horseback for Kansas. The dim wagon ruts led upstream. Shortly after sundown the big moon rose. The lunar light made the rolling prairie a pearl-like outline. Cal turned in the saddle looking around.

"Not much out here is there?"

"Just those coyotes I think are wolves. They give me goose bumps whenever they howl."

"Just company is all they are."

"I wish they'd go be company somewhere else."

"Aw, what would the prairie be like without those sun dogs? The jack rabbits would have little fear and they pull down the old cripples and sick deer."

"You just say those things to make me mad."

"You mad tonight?"

"Mad? Not about what we are doing. I feel we are going after some of the worst criminals in the United States today. They stole U.S. money and lots of it and a cowboy who avoids publicity or acclaim any time he can, along with a very short cowboy and a Choctaw Indian, have outwitted Pinkerton's agents in finding them."

"We got lucky."

"No, you and those two set in to break the case when you got there. The tracks were already cold. They could have gone anywhere. You rode out here and found them. You knew they were here or are in a cat house?"

"Yes, that's where we are going tonight."

"I don't imagine it will be your first visit."

"I'm not going for any purpose but to arrest those two brothers."

"Oh, I'm teasing you."

"There's times I have trouble sorting it out."

"I agree. We neither one have been in a relationship like this in years."

Cal digested it and laughed. "I never have been in a situation quite like we're in right now. I think I'm walking on quicksand."

"Why? We should be having the time of our lives. We aren't kids. Who could we hurt but ourselves?" she asked, throwing her arms out at the night.

"I guess that's why both of us get our guard up once in a while. Inexperienced with anything like it, I'd say."

"Wondering when the bomb will go off?"

"Yes. Will this make her mad? Am I being too personal?"

"California Hankins, you are and will always be one the brightest stars in my life."

"We can't spend the rest of our lives chasing bad guys—I mean if we're going to be together—"

"Go ahead," she said.

"That's it."

"I wouldn't take you away from it. It's your life. You couldn't tend a milk cow and some chickens and be happy."

"You couldn't quit your job as a big city reporter and be a house wife."

Her words were soft and they stung him like lashes from a whip. "No one's ever asked me either."

He simply nodded thoughtfully at what she had just said. It went in like ink blotted by sand.

"Let's see how this goes tonight."

"Yes," she said. "I didn't mean to upset you. I am certain having those two on your mind is enough for anyone."

"Judson and Renton Davis are their given names. I guess one don't go without the other. They've avoided being arrested for years. Like Jesse and Frank James. Still lots of southerners that will hide them, give them horses and money, even give them guns and ammo. These folks really hate the banks and railroads who in turn the outlaws live off of."

"Are these guys twins?"

"I'm not sure. Big bruisers like Homer I imagine. Chief pointed out he was one of them when we rode up, so they must be large blonde guys."

"I really saw the tension build when you told him to disarm. Homer considered drawing on you, didn't he?"

"I thought he would. It was his decision. I was prepared to kill him if he tried."

"Do we have time to stop and walk our horses a ways? I need to stretch my legs."

"I've got all the time in the world for you."

"There you go again." She dismounted, ran over, hugged and kissed him.

He closed his eyes to the moon and stars to savor her sweet mouth. *My heavens where have you been all my life Trudy Staunton?*

Chapter 7

Past midnight he found there weren't many windows in Marlene's cat house. A lamp was on in the front room and the orange glow shown on the window glass beside the door. Over his head the bloomers were slapping the flag pole.

"You stay here," he said, off handedly leaning on the rack where he tied Whiskey.

"No. I've been inside one of these before. I'm going and I'm backing you."

He turned up his palms and then knocked on the door.

"Good evening sir." The woman in a billowing white shift bowed.

"Ma'am at this point," he said seeing the parlor was empty. "I want to inform you that I am a U.S. Marshal and I am here after the Davis Brothers."

The dove sucked in her breath. Plain looking, her brown hair was stringy and her eyes bore dark rings underneath them. She must have poured on a bottle of perfume, it stung his nose this close to her.

"What room are they in?"

"I'm not at liberty—"

"What room are they in?"

"Jud's in ten with Ruby." She pointed down the dim hallway. "They may kill me."

"If they won't, I will. Where's Renton?"

"In fourteen."

Cal held out his hand. "Give me the key to those rooms."

"I—I can't."

"You better."

She reached in her pocket, looking bug eyed at him and gave him a key. "That should open them."

He nodded and spoke to Trudy. "This is where the going gets tough."

Somber faced, Trudy agreed and drew her .30 caliber Colt. "I figured this would be much harder than the ranch deal. I can shoot this revolver."

"Last resort only."

"I understand." And she gave him a head toss to continue.

He paused with second thoughts. *Here were two of toughest outlaws only a few doors apart that had evaded capture by every law enforcement and detective agency in this country for two decades. He was seconds away from arresting the first one of them. Any outburst at all from this one would bring his brother to his aid.*

He switched hands with the key and dried his palm on his pants, then started down the dark hall way. He whispered over his shoulder, "When we get in there try to keep her from screaming."

"I will."

His ear to the thin door of room ten, noting nothing but snoring in there. Motioning her back while he tried the key and the lock gave a small click. Easing the knob as gently as he could, the door opened and he slipped inside the dark room. Starlight flooded the small window.

The snoring hulk of a man was curled around a female in the bed. He sent Trudy to the left and he went to his side. The Colt cocked he stuck the muzzle in the man's face.

"One sound and you're dead."

"Huh?"

"You heard me Davis. You'll be dead."

"You sumbitch, who are you?" Davis growled.

"U.S. Marshal."

Trudy had jerked the groggy dove out of the bed and covered the girl's mouth with her left hand. "Listen to me. You scream you'll get shot."

Even in the room's shadowy light, Cal could see the wide eyed woman nod that she understood the consequences. Things were going his way for the moment but this was only half of it. He put handcuffs on Jud and locked them through the metal bed post so he laid face down on the bed.

"You'll never get away with this."

Not bothering to answer his threats, with his pocket knife he cut off a strip off the bed sheet. Working with his knee planted in the sweat stinking man's bare back to hold him down, he gagged Jud.

"Watch these two," he said to her. Then he leaned over and whispered in Davis's ear. "She'll damn sure shoot you."

Davis nodded and Cal holstered his six-gun. Headed out the doorway, he was blindsided by a fist from a screaming man big as a bear. The blow knocked him down and lucky his attacker was bare footed because he was kicking him and shouting for Judson to come help him.

In the melee, Cal managed to gain hold of one of Davis' feet and twisted it hard enough to send the outlaw to the floor. They both bounced up to their feet and Renton missed a wild punch. Cal charged inside with a powerful upper cut that must have driven the wind out of him. The blow would have stopped an ordinary man. Not Davis.

The outlaw came through a barrage of his fists and bear hugged him. His fetid breath in Cal's face, he roared like an angry bruin squeezing Cal to death. It took two tries but Cal's knees finally drove hard enough into the man's crotch that he let go. That gave Cal a chance to get his arm around the man's neck and drive his head into the door facing. It fell out of the frame from the impact and dirt from the collapsing soddy interior wall flew everywhere.

From the crash, Renton went face down like a poled steer and Cal managed to draw his gun. With his knees in the man's back, he pressed him down. There were screaming whores in various states of dress and undress running everywhere up and down the hallway.

"You need another pair of handcuffs?" Trudy asked, looking hard at him.

"Yes."

"I'll go get them." And she was gone.

Cal's short breath cut like a knife through his throat. His chest hurt from straining with Davis and his ribs were sore all over again. *Damn him anyway.*

"Where's my brother?" Renton asked.

"Handcuffed in bed, right in here."

"Who are you?"

"U.S. Marshal California Hankins, Federal Court Fort Smith, Arkansas"

"You're out of your jurisdiction."

"Kansas ain't out of the U.S. is it? Don't matter. Right now, I have you and your brother and the rest of the train robbers. Where's the money at?"

"How did you ever find us?"

Cal had begun laughing. "Hell you left a trail a mile wide over here. Where's the money?"

"What money?"

"Where is it?"

"Find it yourself."

"I will."

He looked up to see a buxom woman in a low cut dress with her arms folded. "And to who do I owe the pleasure of this meeting?"

"U.S. Marshal Cal Hankins, ma'am. You've been harboring two, much-sought-after, criminals here."

"I never realized it. Thought they were business men."

"They're the Davis Brothers."

"They called themselves the Yarnell Brothers. What will you do with them?"

"I'm sending them and their entire gang to Fort Smith, Arkansas to stand trial for a large train robbery to start with."

"Do you always bust up other's personal property arresting such men?"

"Ma'am, I'd do about anything to catch outlaws like them."

"Here's the cuffs." Trudy handed them to him.

"And who are you?" the madam asked, looking her up and down.

"His flunky." She turned to Cal. "What now?"

"Check that room Renton was in. The loot may be in there."

She nodded and ordered the crowd of curious onlookers to back up so she could go through. They obeyed her.

In a few moments, Trudy shouted. "You have any help?"

"What do you need," the madam asked.

"I need a stout man to carry these carpet bags down there."

"I's going to help her Miss Marlene," a tall stoop shouldered black man said.

"What did she find?" Marlene asked Cal.

"I hope part of the loot they took from the robbery."

"So I have been a bank for highway men this week?"

Standing over the face down Davis whose hands were cuffed behind his back, Cal took the hat he'd lost in the fight from one of the doves. "Thanks. Yes, I guess they bought champagne by the case and fancy food too."

"Some."

"Let us through," Trudy said.

"She your wife?" Marlene asked.

"No, she's my deputy."

"Well. Now that you have these dangerous men locked up, your deputy can watch them and one of my girls can show you some real pleasure."

"No, thanks, but she and I would take some breakfast if you're serving."

"Fine, then if you aren't interested in some real pleasure, we shall eat."

"Someone needs to get word to the local law. Tell them to send a buckboard and some help. That I have the Vinita Train Robbers under arrest."

The woman's face paled. "I read about that. There was—"

"Lots of money was stolen from there."

"Very impressive, sir. I shall send your message to the local sheriff."

"Good," Cal said. "The party is over girls. Go back to bed."

At last he and Trudy were alone, save for the two prisoners.

"Those two bags are full of money," she said, shaking her head and dropping her butt on the bed.

"Good."

"There's still lots to do, isn't there?"

"Lots, but the best one will be sending that telegram to my boss."

"He should be happy. I'll send my story in too. Guess I better get busy writing it."

"Work never gets over does it?"

"Not in this case. Not ever."

Marlene's breakfast was fancy by his standards. Two sullen prisoners eating with handcuffs at a side table. Cal and Trudy enjoyed themselves. They finished in time for the sheriff to arrive.

A large raw boned man in a suit came to the doorway. "What in the hell's going on Marlene—sorry ma'am."

He must have noticed Trudy.

"Those two are the Davis brothers," Marlene said, indicating them. "Marshal Hankins and his deputy, Miss Staunton, also have lots of the loot from the Vinita train robbery."

Cal stood astraddle the chair and shook his hand. "This is Miss Trudy Staunton. Actually she is a reporter for the *New York Times* newspaper."

"My pleasure ma'am and you too Hankins."

"Lidia, bring Sheriff Elms some breakfast please."

"Aw, I can't eat, Marlene."

"There are two things men can always do. One of them is eat," she said with a sly wink at Cal.

"Where do we begin?" Elms asked him.

"Lock these two up. Have some bonded people count the recovered money and keep it in a bank. Then we need to send a party to the K T L cow camp and collect the others in the gang. My men are holding them down there."

The black woman served the lawman a heaping plate of eggs, potatoes, meat and biscuits. "There you go, Mister Sheriff. She said you could really eat."

"Thanks Lidia. Back to your deal, you already have the rest of the gang under arrest?"

"Yes, I couldn't risk anyone warning these two. They're down there."

Fork in his fist, Elms shook his head. "How did you figure all this out?"

"It's my job."

Trudy looked up from Elms to Cal. "And I think he does a wonderful job at it."

Elms agreed with a head shake, no doubt to clear it. "I'll hand it to you. I just read yesterday in the Kansas City paper that the Pinkertons were hot on this gang's trail down in the Indian Territory and would have results in a few days of the arrest of the Davis gang."

"You see any of their agents around here?" Trudy asked him with a wink at Cal.

"No ma'am. I'm sorry I am too amazed to hardly eat."

"Better eat. I need to go telegraph my boss."

"Whew! I'd bet he'll be happy."

Cal nodded. *He better be.*

Chapter 8

Overnight Medicine Lodge became a Mecca of busy people, reporters, bigwigs from Pinkerton and the curious. Trudy had turned her story in and the loot money had been counted at the local bank. Sixty-six thousand was left, counting Homer's ten grand which Shorty recovered at the ranch.

"In three days, they blew that much money?" Trudy asked, over their breakfast in the hotel restaurant.

"No, not all of it, but they had to pay off whoever gave them the information on the shipment too."

"You figured that one out yet?"

"Easy we find out who's spending fresh printed money around Vinita."

"They could be anyone."

"No, this one is a good employee. Lives quietly back there somewhere in a bank or business that knows these things like when the money is coming."

"You have a good imagination."

"Maybe. Look here comes my boss in the front door." He rose to wave Johnson over.

"How are you Miss Staunton?"

"Fine sir," she rose and shook his hand. Cal showed him a chair and waved the waiter over.

"You got a fast train up here," Cal said seated again and cutting his ham.

"I did. I was so shocked to read that wire that you had gotten all of them. This is quick. I can't say how much the entire marshal service is so proud of you and your people. Judge Parker said to commend you for a job well done."

"I still lack one. The informer that told them what train had the money."

"You seriously think there was a person gave them the word? Not some by luck deal that they just happened to get the money train?"

"No. I believed from the start this was a well oiled plan. If it was, I'd like to find the Judas."

"You've got a month with pay to find them. What solved this for you?"

"The brand on the horses, I'd say. Pinkerton would never have noticed if the cowboys Shorty talked to had told them that all the strangers in town before the robbery were riding H T branded horses. Ranch ponies."

"There you go. Miss Staunton did I send you out with the right man?"

"Yes you did. I have been amazed at your lawmen, especially Cal here, and the work that they do."

Johnson ordered his breakfast and then he turned back to them. "I'm starved. It was a heckuva train ride up here."

"I bet it was that. Pinkerton arrived yesterday saying they were taking over this investigation and interrogation of the prisoners."

"Blowhards. What happened?"

"Sheriff Elms told them they were my prisoners and for them to go to hell."

"I like that man already and haven't even met him." Johnson winked at Trudy.

"Oh, yes," Cal said coming back to his own problems. "I am very broke buying and paying for all these things."

"A man about to receive ten thousand dollars in reward money and you're broke?"

"We better lower our voices. There's Charles King. He's Pinkerton's boss man in this deal."

"Good day gentlemen, and ladies too."

"This is my boss, Hal Johnson, Mr. King."

"Charles is my name. Good to meet you. Now you are here, we of course would like to interrogate these hardened criminals and get as much information as we can from them."

"Sir," Johnson began. "You need to contact the prosecutor in federal court in Fort Smith. We don't have the authority to allow you to do that."

"You don't understand. We work hand in glove with the U.S. Marshal Service all across this country."

"Oh, I do understand," Johnson said. "Get permission and you may then interview them."

When King huffed off, they all laughed.

"All that puffed up windbag wanted was someway to get Pinkerton involved in that case that you solved and then use it for their own publicity." Johnson shook his head in disgust.

"We're not done yet," Cal said. "There was an insider that set this up for them." Shorty and Chief talked to each one of the gang members down at the headquarters and learned nothing. The Davis Brothers must have paid him out of the robbery proceeds. So the money is new and fresh. Lots of twenties, crisp as toasted bread. That might provide a trail we can follow."

"You follow it. I am still amazed how you and your men solved this crime."

"Little details and we got lucky."

"Have you seen her story that came out in the newspaper?" Johnson handed him a copy.

"No, but she was sure busy writing it." Cal read the headlines

U.S. Marshall Rounds Up the Gang

The sensational train robbery by the Davis Brothers gang was solved by a hard working U.S. Deputy Marshal California Hankins. Aided by a full blood Choctaw tracker, Christian Horsekiller, nicknamed "Chief," and a real cowboy, Evenrude "Shorty" Broyles, these brazen outlaws were trailed across the endless prairies of the Cherokee Outlet to a cow camp and the other two members of the gang were captured in nearby Medicine Bow, Kansas.

Hankins who works out of Fort Smith, Arkansas and the federal court of Issac Parker is a shining example of the U.S. Marshal service...

"Quit blushing," she said. "I write the truth. Don't I, Marshal Johnson?"

"You really do, Miss Staunton. I promised you a story didn't I?"

"Yes sir. You delivered though my back side got sore chasing it down." Then she laughed. "Well, Cal did you like my story?"

"Mighty powerful. Thanks." He shared a glance with her.

"You must be going next to find the last link," she said.

"I want that individual too."

"When do we leave?"

"On the train in the morning Marshal Johnson, I am sure, can arrange a car for our horses and all."

"Good," she said. "I am just getting accustomed to Spook. Is your Chief going to ride on the train? He acted leery about it yesterday when you brought it up?"

"No problem," Cal assured her. "A few shots of whiskey and he'd whip an alligator."

"I'll have that train car set up in no time," Johnson said.

Chapter 9
Vinita, Indian Territory

Cal met Trudy for breakfast in the Palace Hotel. She looked bright, wearing a fine black jacket and long skirt. The weariness that had shone behind her green eyes days earlier looked recovered.

"Well, what will you do next? I mean, of course, after finding this informer."

"I talked to a man about a grist mill that's for sale in north Arkansas. The water supply sounds sufficient to year round grind grain and there is even enough water power for a saw mill as well."

She looked pained at him. "I can't see you as a miller."

"I'm not giving up my badge, if that is what you are worried about."

She reached over and clutched his forearm on the table. "I am not telling you what to do."

"I know you're right. A few weeks sacking dusty grain and I'd be nuts. But I could hire a man to run it and still make a profit."

"Sounds exciting."

"One thing, during the war they burned the residence down during a gun fight. Must have been some rambling house. It's gone. I don't know how long it will take to rebuild it."

"Why would that concern you? I mean you'll be off chasing killers and pig thieves."

"Not all the time."

"Oh." The waiter delivered their breakfasts next. When he finished serving the large plates of food before them, he promised them more coffee and left.

Cal thanked him and turned back to her. "I mean I don't have a house. It's going to take most of the reward money to buy, get the mill set up and finance the setup. It maybe a while before I can build a suitable house."

"What are you getting at Cal Hankins?"

"Well...I planned to...damn it you aren't helping me one bit."

"One what?"

"Trudy Staunton, I wanted to ask you to marry me. But I don't have a..."

"Well why don't you go ahead and ask me?"

"Cause I don't have a decent house for you to live in."

"Did you ever think how a tent would suit me?"

"But you're a city girl."

"Cal, have I complained one time about the arrangements on the trail of those train robbers?"

He dropped his gaze to all the food. Half sick to his stomach, he shook his head. "I want this to really work. No half assed deal."

"You have no idea how much money I have do you?"

"No. Should I?"

"Cal. Both my parents are dead and the value of my estate as the only child would bowl you over."

"Well, I didn't know that or even suspect it. I mean I ain't a gold digger."

"No. I know that. You are a proud brave man and for that I love you. Will you rephrase the last question?"

"Huh?"

She looked at the tin ceiling squares for help. "Ask me over again."

"Oh. Miss Staunton would you—ah, consider marrying a dumb old cowboy—me?"

"I not only would consider it, I would marry you Cal Hankins."

He collapsed in the chair—entirely exhausted.

"Get up," she whispered standing up.

"Sure. Sure." *What next?*

She leaned across the table ready to kiss him and he kissed her over their breakfast.

"That seals the deal," she said

Lord, there was lots of things he had to learn about women. Might never know them all. He was fixing to get a mill and a wife.

"You better eat," she said breaking into his many notions. "We have lots to do."

Their wedding was performed that week by the mayor of Vinita with all three of her men dressed in suits. Chief even wore a top hat. The Osage Milling became a huge success. With her money they built a large rambling house that overlooked the farm land they acquired up and down Osage Creek.

Sitting in the swing on the large porch watching the sundown burn out with her tucked under his arm, he never could remember ever being so satisfied in his entire life.

"That man you arrested in Vinita that time was the one who told the gang about shipment of money. And they only paid him eighty dollars."

"That's right. He worked as a clerk in the express office and dang near had all that money spent by the time we got back there from Medicine Bow. But he cashed the last crisp twenty with a bartender that Shorty found out about. From there it was easy and when we cornered him he admitted it."

"Judge Parker sentenced him to three years in prison."

"Guess you and the boys are going out again next week?" she asked.

"Shame you can't go."

"Someone needs to tend the business here."

"You ever miss New York and that job."

"No silly. I have a much better job here and besides I have you."

"Well." He pushed his hat back and scratched the top of his head. "That ain't much."

"Why Cal Hankins, I ought to whip you."

He hugged and kissed her. It always worked and it shut her up. He was learning all about women–the hard way. *Better than fireworks, any day! He'd be around for Independence Day next year.*

Thanksgiving with a Mysterious Stranger

Jackie King

Jackie King loves books, words, and writing tall tales. She especially enjoys murdering the people she dislikes on paper. She has published four *Foxy Hens* novellas; a traditional mystery, *The Inconvenient Corpse*; a nonfiction book, *Devoted to Cooking*; and dozens of short stories about women. She lives in Tulsa, Oklahoma in a comfortable clutter of books and papers.

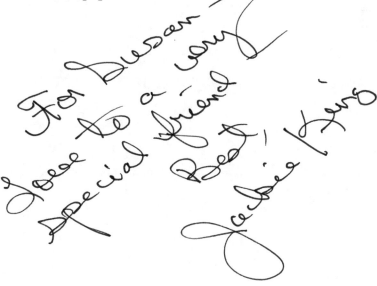

Chapter One
Oklahoma Territory, November, 1889

All Hannah Smith ever wanted was a house with yellow curtains, a small garden and a good cup of coffee. Right now she'd settle for the coffee, but she had only enough grounds for one final pot and she was saving that treat for Thanksgiving Day.

It was her own fault. She'd deliberately annoyed her brand-new husband George, who disliked coffee anyway. Sometimes a woman's mouth opened and words popped out unbidden. And because of that one slip, George swore he'd never again buy her another ounce of coffee.

George loved money more than life itself and had demanded that Hannah turn every penny of her egg and cream money over to him. Hannah figured that if she worked as many hours as George then she should have some say about how their, or at least her money was spent. But he didn't agree, and alas, the law sided with George. A woman had no rights at all.

Marrying George had been a failed attempt toward taking control of her life. Seven months before Hannah had come to the Guthrie Land Run as a mail-order bride. George had advertised in the *Wichita Beacon* for a wife to go with him to the free land run. Sick of her sister-in-law's daily remark about how lucky Hannah was to have a roof over her head; Hannah decided to send a telegram taking the man up on his offer.

Hannah didn't mind that George was 20 years older and three inches shorter than she was. But she hated his stinginess—a sort of blind greed that she now knew was why he had married her in the first place.

The wording in the advertisement stated: "Woman must be shorter than five feet seven inches in height." Since Hannah stood five foot five, she figured she passed muster. Then George Smith turned out to be half a head shorter than she.

"You claimed to be five-foot-five," George Smith accused.

"I am," Hannah answered truthfully, offended at being made to feel somehow defective. To make things worse her sister-in-law and her brother looked on with obvious alarm. The two had been so excited about the prospect of seeing her leave.

"Now listen here, Smith, you promised to *marry* my sister. I have a telegram to prove that. If you jilt poor Hannah I'll sue you for breach of a marriage contract and take every penny you own," Brother said.

"She lied about her height," George protested.

A calculating look filled Brother's eye. "We'll find a judge and ask him to measure each of you and see who is lying."

Humiliation drained through Hannah. "Stop this!" she said. "I'm not marrying any man who doesn't want to marry me. Mr. Smith, you'd better be on your way. I won't be joining you." She turned on her heel and walked back to the kitchen to hide by pretending to sort dried beans.

Ten minutes later the two men joined her. Brother looked smug and Mr. Smith wore a false smile that made her blood run cold.

"The wedding will take place as planned," Brother said. "Mr. Smith is a retired printer who wants to become a farmer. I told him you know all about running a farm."

That was true, but Hannah wasn't about to be bought and sold by anyone, so she opened her mouth to protest.

"Not another word," Brother said. "You're not welcome as a guest in my house any longer."

Guest? This was the house Hannah had been born and raised in and she worked like a frenzied bee to keep the place in order. Aghast, she stared at Brother who refused to meet her gaze. His wife was stronger-willed than he and that made him both ashamed and desperate. A soul-sickness filled Hannah and turned her limp.

The next thing Hannah knew she was sitting on a wagon seat headed toward Oklahoma Territory, legally married to a stranger she knew despised her.

The shame of that day and those following was almost too much to bear. A business deal had been struck between two men—one of whom she thought loved her—and she had been the merchandise. Hannah was certain that Mr. Smith's wallet was thicker when he left her brother's house.

After the cloud of shock cleared, bizarre plans for escape constantly formed in her mind and then were abandoned.

The truth was she had nowhere to go. Women were limited in their choices and men weren't to be trusted.

The morning of the Land Run Hannah had been ordered to stay behind and guard their belongings while George made the run. She longed to have her own horse or mule or even a bicycle to go stake land of her own, but she had nothing.

Along about evening a boy fetched her and guided her to prime land just a mile outside of Guthrie. Hannah frowned. George's horse was very fast, but there had been other fast animals. Then she saw the expression on his face and suspected that he'd come by the place dishonestly. When she spotted a freshly dug grave nearby, her legs grew weak.

"Did you kill someone for this land?" she demanded to know.

"A claim jumper tried to steal my stake. He pulled a gun on me and I was forced to protect myself." George looked her straight in the eye, yet she knew he was lying as sure as God had made little green apples.

***

Hannah sat on the outhouse seat while a cold wind froze her bottom. The privy was the one place she had absolute privacy and could think her own thoughts in peace. She had become accustomed to dawdling there and neither the cold nor the smell could cause her to leave before she was good and ready.

She had brought along her broom because Henry the rooster had different ideas about who ruled the place. Henry seemed to think that his domain included every inch of the hard-scrabble homestead including the outhouse. To level the playing field, Hannah carried her trusty broom whenever nature called, and she wasn't afraid to use the business end to protect herself against Henry's vicious spurs.

The red feathered cock was just one more creature in a long line of males who had made it their business to bully her. First her father, then her brother, and now a pint-sized husband who thought the world revolved around his wishes. Women have no rights, Hannah thought for the umpteenth time. No rights at all!

The sound of horse hooves and then a yell from George brought her out of her reverie. She used a square of newspaper, jumped up and straightened her skirts. Harsh words broke the quiet of the early November morning. Hannah peeked through a knothole in the door to see what was going on.

A bearded man astraddle his horse held a double-barreled shotgun on George. Hannah gasped then pressed a hand over her mouth to stifle any sound.

"You know what I'm here for!" the man yelled. "Hand it over and be quick about it."

Oh! That wretched bankroll George always carried and flashed about. How many times had she warned him? Letting folks know you carried a lot of money with you was not only rude but downright stupid. But George's huge pride, or maybe the lack of it, caused him to stick out his chest and flash a fat wad of greenbacks every time he bought something from the General Store in Guthrie.

"And there's more where that came from," he'd always say.

Hannah would want to sink through the floor from embarrassment. There would always be hard-up farmers with their overworked wives and hungry-looking children standing nearby.

One day Hannah said. "I'll bet that Mr. Smith would love to buy peppermint sticks for all of you children." It was a lie, of course, but she knew his pride would make him treat the poor little ones.

When they got home he had tried to take his belt to Hannah, only she had grabbed her cast iron skillet just filled with frying bacon and told him he'd better not dare—not ever. His lips had grown so thin they disappeared, and that had been the last time George bought her any ground coffee.

Now she was trapped in the outhouse, paralyzed with fear, watching George as he stood with his mouth open. She grabbed the broom knowing it would be worthless as a weapon.

Give him the money! The thought was so strong Hannah feared for a moment that she had shouted aloud. Then George turned and ran toward their hastily built and still unpainted house. One barrel of the shotgun downed him before he was half way there.

The gunman cocked the shotgun, dismounted and took money from George's pocket. He strode to the house and kicked open the door. Hannah studied the distance to the saddled horse, wondering if she should make a run for it.

The idea of being gunned down in the privy made her face burn. Men would laugh when they told that story—even if they felt sorry for her. Such a tale would travel through the country faster than a prairie fire. But she wore her housedress and not the divided skirt that she loved and which George had said to burn because it was indecent. Could she mount the horse and get away before she was shot?

Sounds of pans clanging and dishes breaking rang through the air. The murderer was searching for more of George's money. The cabin was small and he'd soon be outside. She figured he'd go through the barn next and then perhaps the outhouse. It was now or never. She pushed open the door and raced toward the horse, forgetting the broom in her hand. The animal began making a fuss and sidestepped, turning in a circle each time she tried to mount.

The man yelled and stormed out onto the swept yard. He lifted his shotgun toward Hannah who sheltered behind the horse's neck. Then she heard him laugh and the sound sent fear through her heart. A moment later steel-like fingers gripped her shoulder and hot fetid breath made her gasp for air.

Hannah wasn't a woman to go down without a fight. She lifted the broom and brought it down hard. The robber blocked the attack with his arm and laughed again.

"I like my women to fight. You and me is going to have us a little fun, and then I'll decide whether or not to let you live."

Hannah struggled to get even one hand free but he was too strong. To her horror he unbuttoned his filthy-looking trousers with one hand and they fell around his feet. Hannah screamed, but there was no one to hear. The next thing she knew she was on the ground with hurtful fingers pulling up her skirts. She tried to get her teeth into his arm, but he was artful at dodging her.

Somewhere in the heat of the battle Hannah vowed that if she survived this nightmare she would keep her land, prove it up all by herself and never remarry.

A loud squawking filled the air and a blur of red feathers flashed as Henry the rooster spurred the villain's butt right through his longjohns. Hannah's heart leaped with hope and she fought harder. She had no illusions that Henry was coming to her defense. The evil rooster attacked every human that crossed what he considered his domain including the now deceased George.

"Why do you keep such a wicked bird?" Hannah had once asked. "I'd be serving him for Sunday dinner."

"He keeps the hens happy," George had answered.

His words annoyed Hannah. She tucked this crude remark in with all of the other arrogant and tacky words spoken to her by the men in her life.

Henry squawked again and seemed to renew his attack using his strong wings as well as his razor sharp claws. The robber yelled and pulled back. Hannah freed one hand and stuck her fingers in the man's left eye as hard as she could. He screamed again and she rolled out from under her would be rapist, grabbed the shotgun lying on the ground, and aimed at him. She would have pulled the trigger, but Henry the rooster was in the way.

"You worthless piece of...horse manure!" she shouted. "How dare you attack a helpless woman?"

The thief held his left hand over his wounded eye. "You're going to die, woman."

"You make one wrong move I'll blast you to hell and put another grave on this land." She pondered how to manage her captive when suddenly Henry flew at the two of them as if he were tired of intruders in his chicken yard. Hannah took a hasty step backwards and the thief ran to his horse, mounted and raced away.

Hannah lifted the shotgun to fire and then paused. She had only one shell left, and if she missed he'd come back and finish what he had started. Henry flapped his wings and ran at her. She shifted the shotgun to use as a club.

"Take one step closer and you're tonight's dinner," she said, meaning every word.

Henry cocked his head to one side, studied her with his beady eyes, flapped his wings again and strutted toward the henhouse.

It was then that Hannah started shaking. Her arms were so weak she could barely hold the weight of the weapon. Tears streamed down her face, but Hannah ignored the flood, braced herself against the wind, and prayed.

"Thank you Lord for sending Henry to my rescue," Hannah said. "Also, I thank you for my life, my land, and this new shotgun. Amen."

Chapter Two

Josh Savage watched a pretty, green-eyed woman pull back a patchwork quilt to show the lawman a dead man. She wasn't young but she wasn't old either. About thirty maybe. She held her head high and her chin jutted forward as if she expected an attack and intended to bluff her way through. He'd seen this same expression on his mother's face when he was very young. He stepped to better hear and learned that her name was Hannah Smith. He frowned. Smith was the name of the man he'd been looking for.

City Deputy Marshall Ben Daniels asked questions and the woman answered. The killer was both tall and big and had black whiskers, she said. He wore rusty-black wool pants that had seen better days, and a grimy white shirt without a collar. In other words, he could have been one of many wandering adventurers that trailed through Guthrie, and for sure he fit Craven's description.

"Could I direct you to the undertaker's?" Deputy Daniels asked and Josh saw the woman hesitate. Short of cash maybe? More often than not homesteaders skipped a pine box and buried their dead wrapped in an old sheet or blanket. On their own land, of course.

"No sir, I'll take him on back to our farm and bury him there. I just wanted the law to know what happened. That man who killed George is dangerous." Her voice broke and she had to stop and swallow. "Women especially need to be warned of this villain," she said in almost a whisper.

Josh studied Hannah's pale face. There was a bruise on her left cheek. He frowned and wondered what else had happened to this woman.

"You'll be needing a pretty deep hole." The deputy frowned, showing his concern that Hannah might not be up to such a task.

"Yes, I know a body must be buried six feet deep," Hannah said. "I'm well able to dig a hole." Her gaze shot over to the General Store. "First I need to buy some supplies and visit the bank."

"I wish I could go back and help you bury your husband, Mrs. Smith," Deputy Daniels said, "But we're shorthanded here. There's a Federal Marshal in the area, but he's not in town just now. I'll send him out your way when he shows up."

"Thank you, but I intend to hire a farm hand today."

The deputy spoke his condolences and then paused a minute. "It seems like a heartless thing to say just now, ma'am, but I want to mention that you won't have much trouble selling your stake. That's a prime piece of land."

Hannah Smith straightened as if a board had been shoved down her already erect back. A muscle ticked under her eye and she wet her lips before speaking.

"Thank you, Deputy, but I won't be selling. I intend to stay on my land and prove up my claim." Then she turned and walked into the General Store.

Josh frowned and a plan began forming in his mind. He followed her inside where she bought a box of shotgun shells and a pound of coffee and then headed for the bank. Josh knew he'd stand out like a fox in the henhouse in the bank, so he waited outside by his horse. Ten minutes later Hannah Smith came out of the brick and stone corner building. She was white as a ghost and she looked dazed. She walked to her wagon and glared down at the dead body, looking as if she were mad enough to spit. Finally she seemed to pull herself together and stepped up into the wagon, then headed out of town.

What happened? She'd meant to hire a hand but hadn't. Had she tried to borrow money and been turned down? Josh frowned. Or perhaps she thought her husband had an account and the banker wouldn't give her the money. Josh's fists balled. He remembered how his own mother had been treated by men after his father died. Many tried to intimidate her or cheat her out of the little money she had. Others tried to get her to lie with them without the sanctity of marriage. His eyes narrowed at the memory of her humiliation before he mounted his horse and followed the wagon at a distance.

***

Hannah headed the mule toward home. She had known that proving up her land would be hard. Even with the money George had hidden from her in a Prince Albert can and stashed in the barn, life would have been uphill. Now she'd been told the money was counterfeit! Worthless! The banker said if any of the bills she'd used at the General Store was part of this bad money she'd have to make them good. The wagon wheel ran over a rock and her rump bounced hard against the seat, causing her to focus more carefully on her driving. She hadn't had the nerve to go back into the General Store. She'd face that problem another time. Her plate was full enough for one day.

The banker had handed her back nine dollars that he said was good. The money was the exact amount she had earned during the months of selling eggs and cream and milk to the Grand Hotel.

There would be no handyman now. She'd have to try and survive by eating only the root vegetables and the canned goods stored in her cellar until summertime. Grit and determination must get her through. For sure there would be no more coffee. She ought to return what she had just bought, but then they would want their shells back, too. She might strike a bargain to repay the merchant slowly with eggs and milk.

She scanned the clouds gathering overhead and breathed in the smell of rain. Thank goodness the weather was still above freezing; there wouldn't be snow or ice. But Territory weather could change in an instant and that thought made Hannah shiver.

The ground would be hard because they needed rain. Digging a grave would be excruciating. Her heart sank at the work ahead. Not just burying George but also the torturous labor involved in keeping her land. Especially with no nest egg. After a moment she narrowed her gaze to protect her eyes against the wind whipping her hair loose from its pins. She squared her shoulders. Her bottom felt bruised by the bouncing of the wagon, and her heart weighted heavy. She sighed. *I have no choice. Day by day I'll manage or I'll die trying.*

Hannah drove her mule home, unloaded George, washed his body, dressed him in his black suit and wrapped him in the patchwork quilt she had sewn many years ago for her hope chest. She glanced toward the sun that was lower in the sky than she would have liked.

"I may have to finish digging the grave by lantern," she mused, looking out at Henry, who flapped his wings and glared at her from across the farmyard.

She didn't fancy ruining one of her three dresses by climbing down into a grave, so she put on her husband's old shirt and his work trousers and was pleased to see that they fit her just fine except for being a tad short. A few snips with her scissors took out the hems of the legs and made the outfit perfect. Little did she care that the raveled edge showed at the top of her lace up shoes. She grabbed George's old felt hat and pulled it over her head, stuffing her hair up under the brim.

Such an outfit would anger most men, she knew. But there was no one here to see her or to care.

Fifteen minutes later the sound of a horse caused Hannah to drop her shovel and reach for her shotgun. She lifted the weapon and aimed it at the stranger who reined in his mount and lifted one hand in protest.

"Whoa there, ma'am," he said. "City Deputy Marshall Ben Daniels asked me to come out and say a few words over your husband's grave."

The man had a weathered look that spoke of days in the sun and he sat astride his horse as if the two were one creature. Hannah frowned. No preacher she had ever known had ever looked like this fellow. He reached for something and Hannah steadied her shotgun, then she saw what he was holding.

"Is that a Bible?" she said.

"Yes ma'am," he answered, "it surely is."

Indecision caused the shotgun to waver. Bible or not, this man was about the same size as the murdering thief and he had a hard look about him. No whiskers and different clothes, but he could have shaved and changed. She studied his eye to see if it were injured or bloodshot. Suddenly he started to dismount with no regard to her threat.

"Stay right where you are! This shotgun is loaded and I'm not afraid to pull the trigger."

"Even on an unarmed man?" he asked.

Hannah blinked. Sure enough he did appear to be unarmed.

"How do I know you don't have a weapon hidden somewhere on your person?"

The rider's jaw twitched as if he were fighting a smile. "You can't know for sure, ma'am," he said with a straight face. "But you're welcome to search me however you see fit." He raised his arms straight out from his sides.

If there was anything that Hannah hated it was a challenge where the challenger thought she wouldn't have the guts to call his bluff. He faced her, sober-faced as a judge, but there was a gleam of amusement in his dark eyes that made her want to fill his backside with buckshot, if only he'd turn around. This stranger figured he had her calf-roped and Hannah was so mad she thought her ears might pop off her head.

"Turn around!" she ordered. When he obeyed she stepped as close as she dared, knowing that might be a mistake since a man that size could easily overpower her. But she couldn't let some stranger make fun of her on her own land.

Steeling herself, she placed her hand just above his waist. His body was rock-hard, but warm. A shiver ran down her back and made her legs turn liquid. He flinched and then stiffened again, as if her touch had affected him as much as it had her. She pulled her hand away as if from a flame.

***

The woman's gentle touch flamed through Josh Savage. He wasn't expecting such a thing to happen, and the shock of it stunned him. The touch of a woman hadn't unnerved him for years—not since he was eighteen and he kissed Miss Sally Anderson. And that had been a lifetime ago. It was a minute before he dared speak.

"That seemed like a real thorough search, ma'am," he said in an even voice. "Do you feel safe enough for me to turn around now?"

He had his story ready when he rode in. He always carried his mother's Bible in his saddlebags. He had figured this woman wouldn't buy him as a praying man, but it was the best thing he could think of.

Her face reddened and her eyes flashed. She hoisted the shotgun and pressed the barrel against his back. "I think it would be best if you just climbed up on that horse and rode back to Guthrie."

"The sun is low in the west and it looks like a storm is brewing up fast. The two of us could have that grave dug and this man buried before dark. Then I'll speak a few words over him and head for town." Another lie off his tongue, they came so easily these days.

***

Bone–deep fatigue pressed down on Hannah and she knew his words were true. There was no way she could bury George before night, and if it rained hard enough, maybe not even tomorrow. It was cold but not cold enough to keep a corpse from stinking. She hadn't dared part with money for ice to preserve his body. And it would be more proper for someone to say a few words over his body.

"All right, Mister, but I'm hanging on to this gun while you work."

"That's fine, but would you mind pointing it somewhere else? I'm a little worried that you might accidentally pull the trigger."

"Mister, if I shoot you it won't be any accident." But she wasn't sure of that herself, so she lowered the gun.

"The name's Savage," he said. "Josh Savage." He met her gaze and a shiver slid down her spine. Hannah gritted her teeth and frowned. She watched him pick up the shovel, step down into the half-foot deep grave and began digging.

***

An hour later the body lay in the open grave. It was almost dark and thunder rumbled overhead. Josh removed his hat and opened the worn Bible. He thumbed through a few pages and then began to read.

Bless the Lord, O my soul: and all that is within me, bless his holy name.

Bless the Lord, O my soul, and forget not all his benefits:

Who forgiveth all thine iniquities; who healeth all thy diseases:

Who redeemeth thy life from destruction: who crowneth thee with loving kindness and tender mercies;

Amen

Something deep inside Hannah stirred as he read. The tone of his voice astonished her. She had heard many men of God read the Good Word but never had she heard it read with such reverence. She frowned. Could Mr. Savage truly be a praying man? He sure didn't look like one. Too hard, too worldly, and the touch of him sent fire though her veins. Surely this was some kind of trick. There was no doubt in

Hannah's mind that Josh Savage was razor sharp in the brain area.

He closed his Bible and stood quietly with his head bowed.

An inner peace flowed through Hannah as she thought on his words. It was as if someone had poured warm oil over her head and the wonderful glow spread through her entire body. She hugged herself as the unexpected glow of peace radiated through her. She had been wrong! This man must be a man of God.

She had had no feelings for George. First she had struggled to like him and then to tolerate him—but both efforts had failed. Mostly he had just irritated her.

Then suddenly and unexpectedly a grief for his wasted life swept over her and she began weeping—silently at first and then in great hiccupping sobs. It was as if she could see an ineffective little boy, the young man that followed and finally the sour older man who had carved out such bleakness for himself. She wept for the sheer waste of a badly lived human life.

The man across from her stood silent until she finished snuffling and wiped her eyes with the sleeve of her dead husband's old winter coat. Such a breakdown had never happened to her before. She was glad the darkness hid her blush. She felt Savage's eyes upon her and avoided meeting his gaze. He lowered his Bible just as the rain started. Savage bowed his head and she followed suit.

"Lord, I know nothing about Mr. Smith, but You know everything. I figure he made a lot of mistakes since most of us do. Be merciful. And I ask that you help his wife as she sells her farm and returns to her own people. Amen."

Sell her farm? The warm feeling that had swept through Hannah at the reading of the Scripture turned to ice and then to the heat of anger. She would never sell her farm. She would be buried on it! She glared at Josh Savage as the rain began to soak her clothing.

"I will never sell this farm," she said. "Never."

***

Josh saw iron enter her soul when he mentioned selling. What on earth made her think she could prove up this land herself? No woman could and certainly not this one. She had the spirit to do it but not the physical strength. And somehow it seemed his job to convince her of that fact. Also, he needed to stick around long enough to achieve what he'd come to the Territory for.

The rain increased and soon it would be a downpour. His hat protected his head and he peered through a small waterfall cascading over his wide brim. The woman had to be soaked to the skin even through the man's coat she wore, but her eyes were still filled with the fire of fight. Her courage made him like her even more, too much to want to see her felled by pleurisy or the grippe.

"Ma'am, I know you're bound to be afraid of me and I don't blame you for that one bit. But the truth is, you're going to need some help and I'd like to offer my services as a farmhand, at least for a day or two. I'd work for my meals and a bed in the barn."

"You said you were a preacher." Hannah narrowed her gaze and glared at him.

"No ma'am, I didn't actually say that. But my mama taught me to pray as a child and I've kept to that habit." He took a deep breath. "If you need someone to vouch for me you can ask City Deputy Marshall Ben Daniels." The lies kept growing and growing. He just hoped that by the time all of them caught up with him he would have her safely on a train traveling back to her family.

"You can't stay here. Not even if you sleep in the barn." She shivered and it was all that Josh could do not to pick her up and carry her to the safety of the house.

"You'd better get yourself inside the house, Ma'am." Josh gestured toward the shack. He calculated the words he spoke and the effect they would have on this woman. "I'll be heading on back to Guthrie, but I'll be back tomorrow to check and see how you're doing." Wicked flashes of lightning closely followed rolls of thunder. If he judged her character correctly she wasn't a woman who would send anyone into the night in a storm like this one. He watched her mull the problem over.

"Mr. Savage, since the storm is so fierce, you're welcome to spend the night in my barn, and there should be room enough for your horse, too."

"I'd be mighty obliged, ma'am," Josh said.

"Give me a few minutes to stir up a little supper then you can come and get yourself a plateful if you've a mind to."

***

Hannah fought her way through the wind into her small home and stripped off her wet clothes in the dark. *She must be quick before he returned!* A dry chemise went over her head first and then all three of her petticoats. Finally she pulled on her blue wool dress. Because it's the warmest thing I own, she told herself, not admitting that it was also the most becoming.

After lighting the kerosene lamp she built a fire in the iron cook stove. The leavings from yesterday's supper—beans and cornbread—were stored in a wooden box that had once held rifle shells. She was so hungry she could have eaten them stone cold, but a hot meal would be more filling. Soon the aroma wafted from the Dutch oven, smelling mighty good.

She divided the meal, ladling the larger portion into a pie tin suitable for taking to the barn. A minute later the stranger's knock sounded and she carried his meal to the door. The wind almost whipped the door out of her hand, but Josh grabbed it. She saw his gaze sweep around the small shack and something like anger flashed in his dark eyes, but he didn't say a word. Hannah felt heat rise in her face—she figured he was thinking that this was a mighty pitiful home for any human to survive in through a Territory winter. His unspoken criticism galled her and she shoved the plate at him.

"This isn't much, but it's all I can manage until this storm passes. In the morning the hens will have eggs for our breakfast. After that, even if it's still raining, you should be able to make it back to Guthrie."

Josh tipped his hat. "I'm obliged, ma'am," he said.

Hannah spent a miserable night under all of her blankets. The cold seeped up through the straw mattress and she got mad at George all over again. Last summer she'd gradually plucked down and feathers from the live hens. When she'd collected enough to make a feather bed George refused to buy her any ticking and then had sold the feathers in Guthrie.

A scratchy bed, however, wasn't her biggest problem. The thing that worried her the most was the stranger sleeping in her barn. The memory of his muscled back under her fingers kept returning to her mind. Admitting that the memory was a pleasant one irritated the fire out of her so she pulled her shotgun closer. She started every time the boards creaked. Whether in fear or in hope she wasn't totally sure.

Chapter Three

Henry crowed at dawn and bright but cold sunrays slipped golden fingers through the un-caulked cracks in the house. How could a morning be full of sunshine and still be colder than ice? The rain had stopped, thank God. She slipped back into the dress she'd worn last night and laced up her shoes. She never wore the wool for chores, but once again excused her choice in her own mind because of its warmth.

Hannah knotted her heavy shawl around both her head and her shoulders and headed for the outhouse. George had first built the barn, with her help of course, then the henhouse. The two-room unpainted house came last. While she had understood the practicality of this plan, her heart had longed for a husband who would have wanted to put her first. One who would want to add the expense of paint just to please her. She sighed and pushed the thoughts out of her head. George was dead and such nonsensical thinking was for foolish young girls. There was no such man for her, nor would there ever be.

She stepped into the farmyard and saw Josh come out of the henhouse with his hat full of eggs.

"Your hens are good layers, Mrs. Smith," he said with a smile, then studied her and frowned. "You look a mite peaked, this morning. Why don't you rest yourself for a spell and let me build a fire and cook up some of these eggs. I can milk the cow after breakfast."

Hannah's mouth dropped open. She couldn't believe her eyes or her ears. This man gathered eggs and milked cows? George always considered those chores 'woman's work.' *And to cook breakfast?* She'd never heard of such a thing! His eyes reflected an honest concern for her well-being. And his eyes! The morning sun turned them more amber than brown. Certainly they weren't black as she'd thought last night. She had only known self-absorbed men who focused on how she could serve them. Her father, her brother and her husband had all viewed her as someone to make their lives easier. A servant who didn't expect to be paid.

"You going to make the biscuits, too?" she snapped and then bit her lip because her words sounded rancorous and she hadn't meant that. She expected his eyes to darken with anger and his answer to match her own tone. His reply astonished her.

"I could, but you might break a tooth on them." He answered seriously, but she saw a twinkle in his eyes.

She bit her lip to keep from laughing. How was a body supposed to act with such a man? "Humph! I'll stir up the bread while you build a fire in the stove. We'll see about the eggs." Why was she being so hateful? He offered kindness and she took the hide off his back with her tongue. Color rose in her face. Should she apologize? But what if he were trying to trick her?

"There's kindling beside the stove. I'll start the biscuits."

At least I can make him a good cup of coffee, Hannah thought.

***

Josh savored the strong coffee laced with rich, fresh cream. His eyes closed and for a minute he was back in his mother's kitchen. He listened to the gentle movements of the woman fetching more biscuits. What would it be like to have a real home, to wake up every morning with a woman who hummed as she cooked?

The fragrance of fresh biscuits slipped onto his plate snapped open his eyes. She was studying him with her serious green eyes and it took him a minute to speak. The words surprised him more than they did Hannah.

"This is the best coffee that ever slid down my throat," Josh said. "And these biscuits are so light I'm surprised they don't float to the ceiling."

He silently cursed himself for saying such a foolish thing. What was wrong with him? He had to keep to his plan. She was staring at him with her mouth slightly open and she wet her lips with her pink tongue. He shivered. When she spoke he knew that she hadn't calculated her words as she usually did.

"That was downright poetic sounding. How did a man like you learn to talk so pretty *and* to cook?" Her cheeks colored in a most becoming way, he noticed. "My eggs were just like I like them," she said. "I felt downright greedy having two. George always said that one was plenty enough for a woman." She smiled. "I'm right fond of eggs and was pleased to have two."

Josh's stomach knotted. What kind of man didn't feed his woman what she wanted? He'd served her two eggs because his own mother had always eaten only one, and he knew she wanted two. She had never said so, but he had known. A strange tenderness crept through him. Such a woman needed a man to look after her, and not to work her to death with no thanks at all.

His feelings scared the hell out of him. There was no place in his life for a woman. He'd never wanted to be a dirt farmer. His job was to find the counterfeit plates. The grave next to Smith's might be the missing partner. Villains never liked sharing their ill-gotten gains. He was certain the woman hadn't known anything about where her husband's money came from. Somehow he must make her understand the necessity of going back to her family and to safety.

"This is a hard land, Mrs. Smith," Josh said. "There's no way a woman can manage alone. The work is too hard and the land still too unsettled. What happened to your husband isn't that unusual in this country. There will be constant danger for you to face."

Hannah's face froze and her soft lips thinned into a straight line. Her eyes flashed with that temper he'd seen before.

"You think I don't know that? You think I imagine that I'll have an easy life? Rest assured, Mr. Savage, I fully understand what I'm getting myself into. But nonetheless I will never sell. I will prove up my own land and I will be buried here. Whether in the near or in the far future, only God knows."

Her fierce determination and her passionate words moved him. She meant every syllable and nothing he said would change her mind. This fact roused his admiration. *Such a woman!*

"I may starve, but I'll never leave because I have nowhere to go." She clamped a hand over her mouth in horror as if she'd said too much.

The sounds of hooves and creaking wagon wheels brought the two of them up from the table almost as one. Hannah reached for her shotgun and Josh stepped to the door wishing he had a weapon so he could protect her.

***

Hannah gripped the shotgun, but even with a weapon she was glad Josh was there. Just the way he stood in the doorway made her feel better; as if he would stand between her and danger no matter what. For one weak moment she almost handed him her shotgun. Then she blinked hard and bit her lip to bring some sense into her own head.

What was she thinking? This man wasn't her protector. She didn't even *know* him. Hannah frowned and pushed ahead of Josh. She recognized the farmer who had staked a claim closest to her own homestead. Turley, that was their name, Merle and Bernice Turley. The man stepped down from his wagon then reached to assist his wife.

"Heard your man got shot." Mrs. Turley walked toward the house with a big smile on her face. "Fetch them chicken and dumplings, Merle and bring them inside."

Hannah watched the two with an open mouth. "Who told you?" she asked, suddenly feeling suspicious of everyone.

"A fella stopped by at dawn and told us, so I put on the kettle to make you some chicken and dumplings." She smiled at Josh. "Are you a neighbor or a relative?"

Hannah made introductions but no explanation. For one thing, there was nothing to say that would justify the man's presence, and she feared her reputation as a decent woman and as a properly grieving widow would be ruined. But mostly she was tired of explaining her own private business to other people.

Josh nodded to Mrs. Turley and stepped forward with an outstretched hand. "Josh Savage," he said. "I rode in at sunup to make Mrs. Smith an offer on her land."

Hannah blinked. He had lied to save her reputation! Her limbs grew weak with gratitude.

"I was wondering myself if you mightn't sell out," Mrs. Turley said. "But it seems like a right shame after staking out such a fine farm. I figured you'd outlive that man of yours, though. He had a weak kind of look about him that I never quite liked." She straightened and bit her lip. "Oh my dear, I'm a woman with a great big mouth. It were wrong of me to speak ill of the dead and I apologize."

"No offence was taken," Hannah said. "I'm a plain–spoken woman myself." She smiled at Mrs. Turley. "I had just married George before we made the run and we didn't really know one another. I was a spinster and wanted a home of my own." She refused to look at Josh Savage. This was more than she wanted him to know about her, but something about Mrs. Turley made her want to tell the truth. The woman seemed like someone she could trust and God knew that she needed a friend.

"I don't plan on selling my land," she said. "I'm going to stay and prove it up myself."

A huge smile spread across Mrs. Turley's plain face. "Them was the feelings I always got when I looked at you. You're a strong woman, and I greatly admire strong women. Them's the only kind that can make it out here in the Territory."

The Turley's left soon after promising to join Hannah for Thanksgiving dinner on the following Thursday. "I'll bring the pies," Mrs. Turley generously offered. Sugar was a scarce and expensive item on the prairie.

***

By the end of the next day Josh Savage was still sleeping in her barn. She had to admit that he'd been a perfect gentleman and was little trouble to have around. In fact, he had done more than his share of the work and even helped with what was usually considered woman's work; digging potatoes from the winter garden, milking, and gathering eggs. If something needed doing, he just did it—as if he didn't understand the difference between what was supposed to be "woman's work" and "man's work."

As a matter of fact, Hannah herself didn't understand the difference. Work was work as she saw it. But still his manner flustered her—mostly because it was full of charm—and she wasn't used to that. One morning she came in from hoeing weeds out of the turnips and Josh was washing the kitchen floor. He wasn't on his knees as she would have been—he'd torn some old rags into strips and fastened them to the end of an old broomstick.

"What on earth are you doing?" she asked.

"What does it look like?" Josh finished the last patch of wood, stood and carried the pail of water outside to empty.

"That's a mighty interesting contraption you have there," she said following along behind him.

"I'm not a man to get on my knees," Josh said.

"Well, don't throw away that mop," Hannah rejoined. "I'm not so crazy about knee work myself."

***

Thanksgiving was two days away and Hannah was worried about what to serve for dinner. She'd invited the Turley's on a whim and because she wanted to get better acquainted with her neighbors. Now she feared that doing so had been a mistake. All of her hens were good layers but to be hospitable, she needed to roast one for a proper holiday dinner. If she picked the wrong fowl and another hen suddenly quit laying, she wouldn't have enough eggs for both her own use and to sell in town. And what if her cow went dry? Thoughts and questions flooded her brain and her stomach roiled.

"STOP!" She shouted aloud just the moment Josh stepped through the door with a bucket of milk.

"What did I do?" he asked, looking bewildered.

Hannah's face grew hot and she knew her cheeks were bright red. Confusion paralyzed her for a minute. What could she say? Then in desperation she spoke the truth.

"I was talking to myself about something," she said and dropped her gaze. A lie formed on her lips, but somehow the words wouldn't come out of her mouth. She glanced up at Josh who studied her with an expression she couldn't read. She glanced down, longing to pull her apron over her head. Silence filled the cabin for what seemed like the longest time.

"It'll be all right," Josh said quietly. "I promise you that it will be all right."

Hannah pressed her hand hard against her stomach. She might as well tell him the bad news.

"I'll have to make an omelet for Thanksgiving dinner," she said. "I daren't butcher a hen." His quiet demeanor comforted her and she forced herself to smile at him. "Everyone round about our farm in Kansas said my special omelet was the best thing they had ever eaten." That was true, but she always served it for breakfast when company came.

Again there was silence. Finally Josh spoke.

"What kind of vegetables will you be serving? I'm right fond of vegetables. And a pot of beans can't be beat."

Gratitude swept through Hannah. She watched him walk to the dry sink, cover the rim of the bucket with a bit of cheese cloth, and pour milk into a large crock. Cooking ideas sprang into her head.

"I can make an angel food cake! I have extra eggs stored in straw out in the cellar. Maybe a special cake will make dinner seem more like a feast." But what would the Turley's think of not having meat on Thanksgiving Day? Would they be sorry they had accepted her invitation?

"Maybe I should serve that rooster for dinner," she said. But there was no extra cash to buy another, and without a rooster, chickens couldn't be hatched. And Henry had saved her from being ravaged and possibly murdered. The thought of chopping off his ornery head made her stomach knot.

"Serve the old cock right," Josh agreed with a laugh. "He's tries to spur my boots every morning I go to gather eggs." He set down the bucket and covered the crock with a tea towel. "I'll carry this down to the cellar."

"Oh, wonderful. We can use plenty of cream!" Hannah stepped to hold the door open for him, then ran ahead to lift the cellar door. He whistled as he walked down the steps.

It was nice having him around, Hannah mused, knowing that such thinking wasn't wise. The two of them worked well together, each anticipating the other's need without any words being spoken. So different from when George yelled orders at her.

She went back to the kitchen, checked her bread and smiled. Three golden brown loaves were ready to cool. She tamped down the store then bundled up. Time to bury the potatoes Josh had dug yesterday. Once safely under a good layer of dirt in the cellar floor, root vegetables would keep until the summer crop was ready for eating.

Josh led his saddled horse toward her. "I'm checking the fence parameters," he said. "I'll be back by dinnertime."

What will I do when he leaves? Hannah wondered.

***

Josh rode back into the farmyard in time for their noontime meal with four rabbits slung across his saddle. Hannah had been watching for him and her heart took wing at the sight of his broad shoulders. He rode up to the porch and grinned down at her like a boy.

"You ever cook rabbit?" He dismounted and held the rabbits up for her inspection.

"I cook the best rabbit you ever put into your mouth," Hannah said with a big smile. "But I've never skinned one in my life."

"And you won't today. I'll not only skin the rabbits I'll gut them and rub their carcasses with salt before I hang them in the cellar to age. That will make their meat as tender as a young chicken." Josh turned and led his mount toward the barn.

Chapter Four

Where on earth did this man come from? Hannah wondered. Everything about him flustered her and at the same time made her heart sing. Such feelings would bring her heartbreak when he eventually left. Each day they spent together, working, eating, sometimes conversing, was a delight to her.

Conversing! It was the first time such a word had ever crossed her mind in reference to herself and a man. No one except Mother had ever conversed with her. Women and men alike had spoken to her and she had been expected to listen and then to follow directions.

But Josh listened to *her*. At first this had made her edgy and shy, but she quickly grew fond of their verbal parrying. She particularly liked the gentle way he sometimes teased her—with a straight face and a twinkle in his eye. She found herself retorting with snappy responses that before, she had always squashed. Brother had been a serious man with no appreciation for joking. Facetious words always brought her a scolding. Josh understood her dry humor and answered in kind; turning commonplace chores and tedious farm work into fun.

And the rabbits! Without being told he had understood her anguish at the thought of serving a meatless Thanksgiving dinner. He had sought out fine fat game just for her to serve. Rabbit had always been her favorite dish. A special kind of tenderness poured through her like warm honey. Then just as suddenly a chilling thought turned the warmth into solid ice.

Josh would soon leave. Forever!

Her own bleak life stretched endlessly into the future. How had she come to care so much in such a short time? Each hour the bond between them seemed to strengthen. Josh's absence would be the hardest thing she had faced since the death of her mother when she was nine. And he would leave. He was a traveling man.

Hannah pressed her hand over her heart. She must be brave. Josh had been kind to her and she must never let him know how much she cared. Everyone had to live their lives as *they* chose. She would never do to him what had been done to her. She would never force Josh to substitute her dreams for his. Not even if that were possible. She couldn't, she loved him.

Shock resonated through Hannah and she sucked in a hard breath. *She loved him!* She had read about love as a girl in the books Mother brought West; Jane Austen and Emily Bronte and Charlotte Bronte. How she had adored each story! But finding herself single after passing a marriageable age had forced her to accept that love stories were make believe. Such tales were written to entertain lonely women, she figured.

But she'd been wrong. Love was real. And love was wonderful. Hannah closed her eyes and took a minute to savor the magic. Just last night Josh's presence had filled her with contentment and joy. He sat near the stove mending a harness and the soft glow from the kerosene lamp threw a golden light over him. Hannah couldn't keep her eyes off him. The patience and the strength of his fingers delighted her. That special feeling wasn't just friendship, it was love. True love.

And tomorrow he might ride out of her life forever.

The sunburst–feeling inside her chest changed into black clouds with lightening speed. Just like Oklahoma Territory weather. She should never have allowed him to stay. Not one minute. God knew she'd tried to get him to leave, at least at first. She'd deliberately been unpleasant: threatened him, ordered him around and insulted him. He'd just raised an eyebrow, smiled, and then ignored her words.

If she were wise she would order him off her land immediately. He'd have no choice but to obey. And he would obey. He was that kind of man. But could she make herself say such words when she wanted so badly for him to stay? Even a few more days with him seemed suddenly precious.

Her heart hurt. Still, if his absence seemed that painful today, what would it be like tomorrow? Or next month? It was definitely wisest to part now. She chewed on her lower lip.

Or maybe she'd wait until after Thanksgiving. He *had* shot the rabbits, after all.

***

Josh skinned the last rabbit and gutted it, being careful to avoid the sack in the gall bladder. Then he hung the carcass alongside the other three. There would be more than enough game to make a Thanksgiving feast. The look on Hannah's face when she'd told him there was no meat for her guests, had reminded him once again of his own mother's struggle when he was a boy. Anger toward Hannah's criminal husband blew through him.

Just last night he had wondered if Hannah would be willing to pack up and travel on to Texas with him. Then he laughed at himself. Why would a smart, good-looking woman like Hannah want the likes of him? His life would have been a disappointment even to his mother. But God knew he'd tried. After finishing school he had apprenticed with a local lawyer until his mother passed away. That was ten years ago and he was twenty at the time. Studying law had suddenly bored him. One day he saw a flyer in the Post Office offering a reward for the capture of a counterfeiter. The challenge had appealed to him so he decided to track the villain.

He'd been so successful the U.S. Government had offered him a job as a Treasury Man and he'd jumped at the chance. The work suited him and he had continued until he had enough money saved for his real dream: a small spread in Texas. After this job he planned to head south. Now suddenly, something about this plan seemed wrong to him.

Tracking George Smith and Gus Craven from St. Louis to Guthrie had been routine. Smith had owned and operated a small printing shop. Craven had been suspected of stealing an almost perfect set of twenty dollar counterfeit plates from someone in Chicago. Craven had traveled west to escape both the law and the criminals he'd crossed. Soon after arriving in St. Louis he and Smith met. Six months later bad money began circulating in the area.

Now Smith was dead, killed by Craven, perhaps. But if that varmint was still alive he'd come back for the plates. There was no doubt about that. The government wanted both the plates and the counterfeiters. Craven could show up at any time. The thought of Hannah at the mercy of such a man filled him with pure hatred. He'd stayed within earshot of the farm even while hunting game and still had worried about her safety. He had to stick close to her. Luckily, hanging around Hannah Smith was exactly what he wanted most to do. But he knew that wasn't necessarily good.

The lies he had told her to explain his presence had backfired. He often used fake backgrounds to protect his anonymity. But he feared that Hannah would judge him a liar.

Each day this woman and her farm seemed more like home; more essential to his life. He had liked her from the beginning. Now just the sight of her made him happy. But Hannah Smith was a woman who loved truth. When she learned the truth, would she feel tricked? Would she judge him as untrustworthy, as her husband had been?

Once he'd thought of packing his saddlebags and watching the farm from afar. He'd walked into the house to tell her he was leaving and the sight of her stopped him cold. She stood at the kitchen table, elbow deep in bread dough, keeping time to her kneading with the hymn she sang. She glanced up with a smudge of flour on her cheek and a tendril of hair spilling onto her face. She smiled at him. He nodded back, got himself a drink from the bucket sitting on a stand beside the dry sink and left.

He had no business leaving, he told himself. It was his job to stay. Hannah was like a sitting duck. If Craven showed up, he'd rape her before he robbed her. Then he'd kill her before he left. And this time he'd make sure he shot the rooster first.

Thoughts of the rooster made him grin. The damned bird tried to spur him every time he walked through the farmyard. A man couldn't help liking such a contrary creature. Something about the feathered brute reminded him of himself. His boots protected him from injury, but their leather was worse for the abuse. Hannah kept threatening to wring the bird's neck, but he'd noticed she didn't seem tempted to roast him for Thanksgiving. She always carried her broom to the outhouse for protection, but she only used it to shoo him away—never to hit him.

Hannah! His thoughts always returned to Hannah. The woman was a puzzle and he'd always loved puzzles. Each day he wanted to know more and more about her. He'd watched her unfurl a bit each day—like a rosebud. Teasing a smile out of her pleased him. Soon he'd make her laugh aloud.

And the thoughts he had at night! She'd brought him extra quilts to make him a bed in the straw and her thoughtfulness had surprised him. He'd often slept on the prairie, wrapped in a blanket. He wasn't used to a woman fussing over him. But he liked it.

Hannah walked into the barn wearing her dead husband's old coat. She announced she was driving the wagon into town to sell the extra eggs and cream from the cellar. He tried his best to talk her out of it, but she wouldn't budge.

"It's only a mile to town," she said, "I must see the grocer."

He couldn't leave the house. It was his sworn duty to stay where he was and wait for Craven. Josh's belly hurt. Women! Weren't women supposed to be helpless and pliable?

And damn, he hated that coat. Soon as he got to town he'd buy her a decent one whether she liked the idea or not.

***

Hannah drove her wagon into Guthrie. Five dozen eggs packed in straw and a half-gallon of cream braced in a front corner stood ready to trade against her General Store debt. She wished she could peddle them at the Grand Hotel. Harriet Lauren, the owner, always paid more and her helper Radine Morgan was fun to visit with. But she had a debt and she must try to settle it in the only way she could.

Hannah dreaded facing the businessman, but it had to be done. His tight-lipped scowl softened as she explained her problem, and he agreed to her suggestion of a gradual repayment with eggs and cream. Hannah figured there was a big need for such items, especially right before Thanksgiving.

Dare she spend thirty cents to buy a pound of coffee? She decided she must. Skimping on coffee at Thanksgiving was unthinkable. The cash purchase brought a smile from the store owner.

***

Hannah was more than halfway home when a she heard a horse pulling up fast from behind. She glanced back and fear shot through her. The rider had black whiskers and a patch covered his left eye. Dear God! George's murderer had returned for his revenge.

"Gee Haw." She snapped the reins and for the first time in her life wished she owned a whip. Her mule stepped a little faster, but the rider was already racing along beside her. Her heart pounded in terror. *Why didn't I listen to Josh?* She wondered.

"Whoa, there." The male voice was gruff and angry and she sometimes had heard it in her nightmares.

A meaty hand reached down to grab the mule's reins. Hannah doubled one of the straps and used it to flail at his hand. He laughed and the evil sound almost stopped her heart. Then his heavy body slid from his saddle onto the seat beside her. Hannah angled her body toward him and kicked with all her might, aiming at his groin. He swore and ripped the reins from her hands then leaned back and jerked on them.

"Whoa!" he yelled. "Whoa, you damned animal."

The mule tossed his head and Hannah knew from experience that old Buster was riled. But he was a well trained animal and would finally obey. But maybe his hesitation would give her the chance she needed.

Hannah reached for the shotgun leaning beside her. She was too close to aim but she used the gun as a club and swung the double barrels at the rapists' head. He caught the weapon with one hand and pushed the barrel skyward. Hannah's finger made purchase with the trigger and she pulled. One barrel fired but missed her target. Her enemy pulled the weapon away with a roar of anger.

"I'm gonna teach you to blind a good man, Missy." Hot breath made foul by rotted teeth and chewing tobacco gagged her. "Think you're too good for me, don'tcha?" His voice lowered to a sneer. "Before I slit your throat I'm teaching you a lesson just behind that there cottonwood tree."

Chapter Five

Josh shoveled manure from the barn into a wheelbarrow. He'd spent the morning cleaning the floor and making a compost heap in the garden. The sound of a shotgun blast echoed, sounding as if it came from about quarter of a mile toward Guthrie. He dropped his shovel and in one swift movement bridled his horse, mounted barebacked, and raced toward the sound. Too late he remembered his gun in his saddlebag, but there wasn't time to go back. He had to save Hannah.

Sweat lathered his horse by the time he heard Hannah's screams. He raced toward the sound of her voice, too scared for her safety to worry about his own. He crested a small rise and saw that a man held Hannah to the ground with his right hand and held a knife at her throat with his left.

Josh reined in his horse and the man shouted, "Stay out of this cowboy. This here is none of your business. Interfere and I'll kill this woman and you, too."

"I might be a mite hard to kill." Josh slid off his horse. He recognized Craven from the drawing sent by the Treasury Department.

"Get on your horse and ride out or I'll cut her throat," Craven shouted.

"Do that and you'll die *real slow*." Josh braced himself, ready to spring. He could take the man, but in the instant before he reached him, Hannah might die.

Craven's eyes said he was ready to make his move. He released Hannah and reached behind him for what Josh figured was a gun. In that instant Josh leaped forward, hoping Hannah would have the presence of mind to roll away and run.

The brute pointed the knife at Josh's belly and lunged. Instinctively, Josh twisted, barely missing being gutted. Josh grabbed Craven's left wrist and forced it upward while struggling to pin the hand holding the gun. He'd miscalculated the man's strength.

A firearm sounded and what felt like a cannonball ripped into Josh's chest. The wetness of his own blood soaked his shirt. He heard Hannah run to the wagon. Thank God. Now if only he could stay alive long enough to keep Craven busy until she got away. There were worse ways to die than protecting the woman you cared about. He listened for the sound of wagon wheels. Why wasn't she driving away? He didn't know how much longer he could grapple with Craven. The pain seemed blinding and he feared he'd pass out from loss of blood. Craven shifted and kneed Josh in the groin. Agonizing pain paralyzed him and the scream he heard was his own.

***

The knife slacked away from Hannah's throat and she rolled away from her attacker. Her limbs trembled so fiercely it was a struggle to stand. She saw Josh wrestling with the killer who held a weapon in each hand. Josh had nothing but his own courage. *I must save him,* Hannah thought.

She ran to the wagon, grabbed her shotgun and hoisted it to her shoulder, but the wrestling men kept her from a clear shot. Suddenly the villain kneed Josh in his privates and he screamed then collapsed to the ground. Hannah steadied her aim and fired the last barrel, catching the varmint full in his chest. She'd been aiming at his head, but no matter. A look of astonishment spread across his evil face then he fell to the ground.

Hannah ran to Josh, terrified at the amount of blood he'd lost. His face was white but his eyes sought hers.

"Hannah," he whispered. "My cherished one."

Then his eyes closed.

"Josh!" Hannah shouted. "Don't you dare die on me."

She pulled off her petticoat and tore off the ruffle at the bottom, then pressed a large piece of the front panel against his chest. She must staunch the flow of blood. The cotton pad quickly turned red and she ripped another length and continued the pressure. Blood seeped through, but slower.

"Thank you Lord," she breathed, and then tore the ruffle twice to use as binding for the pad. She tied the strip tightly. Should she take him back to Guthrie to a doctor? She feared he'd never survive the trip. Her house was closer. If she could manage to get him into the wagon it would be safest to take him there. Somehow she would keep him alive.

Josh shivered and Hannah slipped George's heavy coat from her shoulders and covered him. She fetched water from a jar in the wagon and bathed his face. His eyelids fluttered.

"Hannah," he said. He even smiled.

"You're going to be fine," she said in a firm voice that surprised her. Her hands shook along with her whole body—but somehow she kept her voice even. That was good. She didn't want him losing hope. "I've got to get you into the wagon. If I don't the bleeding will start again, so you must lean heavily on my shoulder and let me do most of the lifting. Do you understand, Josh?"

His lips twitched and then curved into a smile. "Reckon you could lend me your shotgun to use as a cane?" he asked.

"Oh, yes. If you promise not to start bleeding again," Hannah murmured the words against the side of his face.

"Yes, ma'am, I'll do my best."

***

Getting Josh back to the farm seemed to take forever. Hannah settled him into the wagon bed and drove slowly. But she knew he must have suffered agony. She pulled the wagon as close to the house as possible and somehow, with his help, managed to get him inside. She put him in her own bed and went to the kitchen to ready things. There was no one to send for a doctor and she daren't leave him long enough to ride to the Turley's farm.

Hannah filled a pot and boiled her sharpest knife along with a good long length of white linen thread. After locating the last of George's whiskey, a wooden spoon, and all the rags she could find, Hannah sat beside Josh and prayed silently until the knife and thread were well sterilized.

"Don't think about what you're doing," Josh said, before he swallowed some of the whiskey. "Pretend you're coring an apple."

If Hannah lived to be a hundred she knew that she'd never have to face a harder task than digging a bullet out of Josh Savage. She folded her hands under her chin, closed her eyes and silently prayed. When she opened them Josh said, "Amen." She gazed into his eyes and forced a smile. Then she steeled herself against the task at hand.

"Don't think, just do it," Josh said. "Pay no attention when I yell. If you stop it'll hurt worse. This isn't new to me and I'll guide you. Now give me that spoon you brought in." He bit into the spoon and directed her with the handle clenched in his teeth. His words were garbled but articulate enough to understand. He groaned between instructions but she refused to think of anything except extracting that poisonous bullet.

***

When the task was finally over Hannah went limp with relief. Every rag plus a couple of her clean towels were blood soaked. She poured the last of George's whiskey over the wound, stitched the edges together and bandaged the ugly slash with a pillow case. Josh was white and his eyes were closed. Was he conscious? She held a small bottle of ammonia under his nose. He stirred, his eyes opened and he glared at her.

"What are you doing, woman?" he asked, "God in Heaven. Haven't you tormented me enough?"

She sighed with relief and grinned at him. He was alive. She hadn't killed him!

"That was nothing like coring an apple," she said with mock severity. "Men are such liars."

"Nearest thing I could think of," he answered with a wan smile. "I knew you could do it. In fact, I don't think there's much you couldn't do if you set your mind to it."

Hannah thought she might melt in the warmth of his gaze. No man had ever looked at her with such tenderness and…She swallowed involuntarily. What else did she see in his eyes? Was it just gratitude?

"I couldn't have managed without your directions." She smoothed a lock of hair back from his eyes. He reached for her hand then flinched. Fear shot through Hannah.

"You must quit talking and try to rest." She remembered the danger of shock and hurried to her chest to grab a comforter she'd stuffed with goose down two years before.

"This will keep you nice and warm. Do you need anything else? A sip of water maybe?"

Josh frowned and she could swear he looked disconcerted. "I am thirsty," he said. "But first I need you to help me out to the privy."

Being reminded of nature's necessities nonplussed Hannah and she paused for just a moment. Then commonsense rescued her from embarrassment.

"If you even try and walk anywhere you'll bleed to death. I'll bring the privy to you." She reached under the bed for her enameled chamber pot. "This is what you'll use," she said. "And I'll help you. This is no time for nonsense." She spoke in the same tone she would have used with a five-year-old boy.

Chapter Six

Hannah hummed as she began evening chores. She was tired, but it was a pleasant kind of tiredness. The day had gone well, Josh had sat up in bed that day and by tomorrow he might be able sit at the table for Thanksgiving dinner.

She fed and watered the chickens and smiled to see that her "girls" had made their best effort. She praised each one by name but shooed Henry away with the edge of her broom. He squawked and flapped his wings then danced a few 'see-my-spurs' steps as if he were trying to intimidate her.

"The hens may be impressed, but I'm not!" Hannah scolded. "Don't think that I won't plop you into a pot for Thanksgiving Dinner. No reason why we can't have both rabbit *and* chicken."

Henry protested with one last squawk and a few more show–off wing flaps. Hannah smiled, and for no reason at all she kept talking to the rooster.

"Yes indeed, I'm having a special Thanksgiving dinner tomorrow for the neighbors. I may cook all night. When the Turley's come in the morning they'll be welcomed by delicious smells coming from the kitchen."

After the cow was milked and the livestock fed and watered, Hannah went inside to check on Josh. He snored softly. She went into the kitchen and began to cook as quietly as she could. Hannah wanted to make the game dish as fancy as possible. She cut the rabbits into serving pieces and dropped them into salted water for a couple of hours to drain the remaining blood.

She sliced a loaf of the bread she'd baked yesterday and spread the pieces in a shallow pan to dry. Then she stirred up a pan of cornbread to add to the bread crumbs for sage dressing. This was going to be a feast! After the rabbit had soaked for a couple of hours she dropped some of the pieces into a pot of boiling water. Rabbit broth would be just the thing to get Josh back on his feet. Next she wrapped the remaining pieces in a damp cloth and carried the meat back to the cellar until tomorrow. Last of all she separated a dozen eggs and beat the whites into stiff peaks, folded in the dry ingredients and put the angel food cake in the oven. She'd save the yolks and scramble those in the morning for breakfast.

The clock's hands pointed to ten by the time Hannah sprinkled seasoned bread crumbs into a cup and ladled broth over the top. The fragrant aroma pleased her. Holding the cup in one hand and the kerosene lamp in the other hand she walked into the bedroom.

***

Josh opened his eyes at the sound of Hannah's soft footsteps. The homey sounds and the delicious smells drifting in from the kitchen made his stomach rumble. He could tell he was mending fast. Yesterday he'd had no appetite but now he was ready to eat.

"Something sure smells good," he said.

"I made you broth," Hannah said.

"Broth? I was hoping for a hunk of that meat."

"Maybe tomorrow. I'm going to bake rabbit along with some cornbread and sage dressing for Thanksgiving. The Turley's are coming, remember? If you feel up to it you can eat rabbit then."

"Thanksgiving dinner? You don't have any business cooking for company. Good lord, woman, you've been through hell. You have black circles under your eyes and look exhausted. Put on a pot of beans for those folks."

"Thought you wanted a hunk of rabbit?" Hannah sat in a chair beside the bed and shot him a saucy smile.

"What I really want is for you not to work yourself to death." The sounds of her doing the evening chores all by herself bothered him. He'd considered getting up, but when he rolled to his side to try, pain cut through his chest and stopped him.

"I *want* to cook dinner," she said. "I'm making the most wonderful Thanksgiving feast anyone ever ate! I have it all planned." She pulled a straight-backed chair close to the bed, placed a tea towel over his chest and held a spoonful of soup to his mouth.

The broth was the best thing that had ever slid down his throat. He closed his eyes to savor the rich flavor. "What *is* this? It can't be rabbit soup."

Hannah laughed and the sound of the rich, robust sound had been worth waiting for. "Course it is. I just added some spices that I grew and dried last summer and a bit of my dandelion wine."

He could have fed himself. He'd had worse wounds and had managed on his own. But if she knew that, she'd move away and he liked having her close. Liked her smiling down into his eyes in the silent room. There seemed to be no need for words, now. Again and again she dipped the spoon into the cup and then held the broth to his lips. The last time the spoon was empty, but he took it into his mouth anyway. Hannah looked down into the cup.

"Oh, my goodness, you've eaten all of the soup. Would you like more?" She smiled and her cheeks colored prettily.

"Maybe later." Josh reached for her hand, appreciating the touch of her fingers, which were work-worn, honest and warm. "You saved my life."

"And you saved mine."

A tendril of hair fell over her face and she tossed her head to flip it away, all the while smiling at him. Hope rose inside Josh's chest. *She hadn't removed her hand but had left it resting in his!*

Need for her blew through him, and for a minute he couldn't speak. Desperately he wished there were no secrets separating them. Wished he had accidentally stumbled onto her farm while she struggled to bury her husband and he had stayed for the right reasons.

Who would have expected to find a woman like Hannah in this barren country? A woman with courage and good humor and tenderness, a woman who would work beside him, who would fight for him and even assist him in the most personal ways without making a fuss or seeming disgusted? She was a natural born pioneer, a natural born nurse, a natural born mother.

Josh sucked in his breath. Where had that thought come from? And suddenly he knew he wanted this woman for his own. And that he must fight to win her. He had to tell her who he really was and he had to do it now. But she was smiling at him so sweetly that the words just wouldn't form on his lips. Better to think about how to word what had to be said.

"You're different from any man I've ever met." Her cheeks colored again. Her voice softened to a whisper. "I'm glad you came to help me bury George, and that you stayed."

"No man is totally honest," he said. "I've stubbed my toe just like everyone else. Make no mistake about that."

The smell of her almost undid him—soap from a recent wash, the fragrance of bread baking and that special essence of Hannah herself—knotted in his gut like a fist. He longed to possess every inch of her body. How was he going to leave her behind?

Hannah laughed again and he savored the sound. She didn't laugh like most women. Her laughter seemed to come straight from her belly.

"I didn't mean that to be a joke." He couldn't let her think he was joking or being modest.

"I wasn't laughing at what you said. I..." She pressed her fingers against her mouth to stifle her chortling. "I assure you that I've not put you on a pedestal. We have shared circumstances too intimate for that."

Josh, who hadn't blushed since he was sixteen, felt heat flame into his face and spread through his whole body.

That damned chamber pot! Was that what she thought of when she looked at him? He glared at Hannah. Had the woman no decency?

***

Hannah slapped her hand over her mouth. She couldn't believe she'd said such a thing. *Gracious! She'd made him blush!* What had come over her? Yet she felt no remorse and had to bite back a giggle. She knew that if she could, her conscience would require her to snatch back what she'd said. For once in her life, Hannah was glad that she couldn't un–speak words.

She stole a glance at Josh through her eyelashes. He was looking at her and he was grinning.

"Why Hannah Smith," Josh said with mock seriousness. "I'm surprised at you."

She giggled. Had she ever before giggled? Not since she was a girl, for sure. Everything was so comfortable with him. A lifetime of self–censorship just seemed to have melted away. Any foolish thing that came out of her mouth seemed to amuse him. Ordinary life had suddenly become fun.

"I'm sorry I made you blush," she said naughtily, then picked up the cup and the dishtowel and sashayed into the kitchen. Sashayed? She hadn't realized she knew how to sashay. Things that had seemed impossible before were now coming naturally. Like flirting. She was flirting!

Brother and his wife had spoken harshly about young women who flirted with men. Not that any of the young women cared. But she suddenly realized that in her usual attempt to keep herself from criticism, she had ensconced herself in an impenetrable armor of primness. Perhaps that was why no man had ever dared to court her. When had that brittle shell disappeared?

Suddenly Hannah felt vulnerable and defenseless. *Was she making a fool of herself?* The rainbow-colored bubble of happiness popped and disappeared. What have I done? She wondered. Will he think that I'm fast? Men had no respect for fast women, she knew.

Hannah put water on to heat so she could wash the dishes dirtied by her cooking. Then she'd use the water to scrub the floor. Anything to stay busy and have an excuse not to face Josh. She stopped, nonplussed. But if the floor was wet where would she go until it dried? It would be impossible to step into the room where Josh rested, and it was freezing outside. She glanced at George's heavy coat that was hanging by the door. She'd been wearing that and she could put it on and sit on the porch. Freezing would be good punishment for speaking so foolishly.

***

Hannah used the homemade mop that Josh had cobbled up to wash her way to the front door. Then she donned the coat and wrapped her head in her shawl and stepped outside. She propped the mop on the porch and hunched her shoulders against the icy bite of winter.

She'd lived with loneliness all of her life, yet prior to meeting Josh she had never even noticed the empty feeling. She'd preferred being alone to the company of most of the people she knew. Now she felt unexpectedly bereft. Tears stung her eyes and her whole body ached with misery. She stared up at the stars. How could she face the rest of her life without Josh?

The door open and Josh braced himself in the doorway, his tall frame outlined by soft lamplight. He'd wrapped a blanket around him and wore woolen socks. The top of his long-johns showed above the quilt and somehow his state of almost-undress made Hannah aware of her nether-parts.

"What are you doing out in the cold, woman? You'll catch pneumonia! Get back inside!"

"Me? What about you? Standing there in your underwear and your socks? You shouldn't even be out of bed, much less walking outdoors in the night air." She bit her lip. Why did she shout? A sharp tongue never made any man hang around, even she knew that. She dropped her gaze, feeling miserable.

When Josh finally spoke his voice held his usual note of humor.

"Maybe you should *help* me step inside so we can yell at each other in the kitchen where it's warm. I suddenly feel light-headed."

Hannah looked up and saw that his face had blanched to the color of salt. She rushed to support him, but she still spoke in a sharp-edged voice.

"Don't you dare faint out in the black of night! No way could I lift a big man like you and carry you back inside." She wrapped her arms around him to support his weight and they struggled to get back inside. His heart drummed against her body and his breath fanned her forehead.

"Yes, ma'am. Sorry to be such a bother," he said softly.

Josh's body pressed against hers and it was Hannah's turn to go lightheaded.

"Can you make it into the bedroom?" she asked in a hoarse whisper.

"Not sure. Let me sit for a minute in a chair."

They walked slowly to the kitchen where he collapsed into a chair by the table. He grunted with what Hannah knew was pain.

"Have you started bleeding again?" she asked.

"I sure hope not. I know that you have a rule against bleeding, so I wouldn't dare."

Hannah smiled in spite of herself. She couldn't help it. Here she was, scared to death for him, and yet he acted like a fool with his teasing. Who could resist such a man?

"Let me look at that wound and be sure." She slipped the blanket off his shoulder and began to unbutton the top of his long-johns. He sucked in a hard breath and she jerked her hand back.

"I'm so sorry, I didn't mean to hurt you."

***

"You didn't," Josh said through clenched teeth; there was no way he could tell her what he was feeling. Unfastening his button had almost undone *him*. He had wanted to pull her into his lap and kiss her long and hard. He knew he wasn't good with words but he wished he were. And before he could even think about courting her, he had to confess who he really was and why he had come to Guthrie. "There's something I have to tell you, Hannah."

"Whatever it is can wait until I have you back in your bed." She already had his top open to the waist and was checking his bandage. "I'm glad to see that you've obeyed my rules." She said with a smile then fastened up his clothes. "Do you think you can walk back to the bed?"

"I do." Josh reached for her arm, grateful for the cover of the blanket.

"Don't try getting out of bed again without me there to help."

Josh started to say that he'd been wounded worse and had survived, but wisdom stopped him.

Once again he leaned close to the soft temptation of her body. Maybe he should recover more slowly than needed. He could get used to Hannah's tender nursing.

After getting settled back in bed, Hannah softened to his plea for more food and brought him some rabbit and a couple of fried eggs. Nothing had ever tasted better to him, and her sitting in the chair close by, humming while she mended, something made the night almost perfect. If he confessed, she might get angry and go back into the kitchen.

Maybe he should wait until after Thanksgiving? She'd worked so hard cooking, and she'd set her heart on everything being perfect. Maybe he should wait until Friday. Yes, that's what he would do. At least he'd have one perfect Thanksgiving Day to remember forever.

Chapter Seven

A fierce longing swept over Hannah. She wanted to crawl into bed beside Josh and snuggle as close as possible. She had no intention of giving in to her impulse, yet she enjoyed thinking about it.

Josh handed her his empty plate and struggled to sit up.

"Make me a pallet on the kitchen floor," he said. "You need to sleep in your own bed tonight. It's too cold for you to sleep on the floor."

"I'll do no such thing! I've not been shot. You need the bed worse."

"Wounded or not, I sleep on the ground and under the stars more often that I sleep in a decent bed," he said. "I want you to have a good night's rest."

"I have an extra straw tick I can pull down from the rafters. I want to be close to the stove, anyway. I'll be up before dawn to begin cooking. It's Thanksgiving, you know. Then we'll see about tomorrow night."

He opened his mouth to protest but Hannah stopped him by raising her right hand. "I'll have no more nonsense out of you tonight, Josh Savage," she said in a very spinsterish voice. "I'm plumb worn out with arguing with you and I need to get on with fixing our big dinner."

Josh once again opened his mouth and she scowled at him. He grinned back.

"Yes ma'am," he said and she rewarded him with her smile.

She stepped back into the kitchen and began peeling potatoes after she put the turnips into water to clean them.

***

Hannah was up before Henry crowed. She quickly dressed, pulled on George's coat and stepped outside. She could see that it would be a perfect Thanksgiving Day! Cold and clear with blue skies and bright sunshine. She rushed through the outside chores: feeding the chickens and livestock, gathering eggs and milking the cow. Finally she carried in extra wood for today's cooking.

The Turley's wagon drove up about 10 o'clock. Josh had insisted on getting up and he sat at the table. Hannah threw a shawl around her shoulders and stepped outside to greet her friends. Wonderful smells of freshly baked pies wafted from the wagon along with something extra. Ham! Mrs. Turley carried a baked ham.

"Oh my goodness, you brought more than your share," Hannah said.

"I always do," Bernice Turley grinned, showing a missing tooth. I love baking, and this way we'll both have plenty of leftovers." She set the ham on the kitchen table and spotted Josh. "Why Mr. Savage, nice to see you again, how are things in Guthrie?"

Josh stood to greet her. "Morning, Mrs. Turley" he said, then leaned against the table for support.

"What on earth has happened to you? You been hurt?"

Mr. Turley walked in with the pies and joined the conversation. "You have an accident, Savage?"

Josh thought a minute, trying to figure out how to explain things in a way that would cast no shadow on Hannah's character. He was surprised when Hannah herself began to speak, telling the story in a straightforward way. Josh watched the older couple listen to the simple facts. He couldn't read their faces and that worried him. As soon as Hannah finished he spoke.

"The body needs to be taken in to the law in Guthrie," Josh said to Mr. Turley. "I was in no shape to lift him into the wagon at the time, and he was too heavy for Hannah. I was wondering if you'd go with me while the ladies finish their dinner preparation?"

"You can't ride into town, not even in a wagon," Hannah said. "You ought not to even be sitting at the table."

Josh watched the Turley's exchange a glance. Without a word the two seemed to communicate an unspoken message. Mrs. Turley nodded at her husband and he turned to settle the problem.

"It's only a mile into town. I'll drive the wagon over, take the body into town, and talk to the marshal. The law can just as easily ride out and talk to you'uns tomorrow about what happened. No need to disturb our nice Thanksgiving."

"That's a fine plan." Mrs. Turley nodded in agreement. "And when you get back we'll all enjoy Thanksgiving dinner."

"Thank you," Josh said. "I appreciate that."

***

Hannah smiled at the Turleys. What nice people they were. It never occurred to them to blame a woman herself when some man tried to attack her. And Hannah had feared such a response from her neighbors. Harsh judgment against a woman in such circumstances was common.

She glanced at Josh and caught an unguarded expression on his face. He noticed her eyes on him and quickly masked his feelings. But Hannah knew what she had seen. Why was he looking so worried?

"You're not bleeding again, are you?" she asked.

"I'm fine." Josh forced what seemed to Hannah to be a false smile. "Turley's plan is a good one. That man won't be any deader by tomorrow."

Turley guffawed his approval.

"You need me to come along and help?" Mrs. Turley asked her husband.

"No need at all. I know the spot that Mrs. Smith described. You ladies stay here and keep rattling those pots and pans. When I come back I'm going to be hungry as a bear."

Hannah smiled and glanced at Josh, whose drawn face stopped her. She frowned. He was worried! Why?

Chapter Eight

Josh steadied himself against the door jamb and watched Turley's wagon roll away. He had to tell Hannah who he was and why he had come to Oklahoma Territory before tomorrow. The local lawmen already knew who he was and would keep no secrets for him. But it seemed a shame to spoil the day she'd looked forward to and had worked so hard to have. He'd wait until after the Turley's went home this evening. Hannah's voice from the kitchen interrupted his thoughts.

"Come back inside, Josh, you've been up too long. Why don't you lie down and rest for a spell?"

"No thanks. I'm fine. Fresh air is what I need. Don't stop your cooking, everything smells too good. I'll be fine."

"Don't stand too long," Hannah said, but he closed the door between them pretending he hadn't heard.

Mrs. Turley's hearty laugh traveled through the thin wood, as did her words.

"Do I hear wedding bells?" Mrs. Turley said, and Josh could imagine Hannah's blush.

"Hush! He'll hear you! We've only just met," Hannah said. "Mr. Savage is a kind stranger who saved my life. I'm sure he'll ride on as soon as he's able."

"Humph!" Mrs. Turley said. "I know a smitten man when I see one."

Josh took a few uncertain steps into the yard, wishing he'd brought the mop handle for support. He hoped to goodness that Hannah didn't know he'd heard. It bothered him to think of her being embarrassed on his account.

The door opened and closed behind him. He turned. Mortification was burning on Hannah's cheeks. For a minute he considered playing dumb and pretending he hadn't heard, but knew that Hannah was too smart for that. She'd know he was lying. The only thing that would work with this woman was the truth. But what should he say?

"You heard every word!" Her cheeks burned red as fire. "I sure hope that didn't embarrass you, Mr. Savage," Hannah said.

Suddenly Josh knew how to make her feel better. "Not at all. Only one woman has ever made me blush, and that woman was you, Hannah." He smiled.

"Oh." She dropped her gaze and a tiny smile curved her lips. "You're thinking of the chamber pot, I guess."

"You guess right. You're not the first nurse I've had. I've been shot before. But you're the first one that I ever cared what she was thinking."

"You've been shot before? More than once? Oh, Josh. I know nothing about your life before you rode in here."

"I want to tell you all about my past, but now isn't the time. We'll talk tonight after our company has gone."

Hannah looked at him with eyes as green as a June meadow. A need to take her in his arms welled up from his belly, almost overwhelming him. He opened his mouth and spoke without thought.

"Mrs. Turley was right," he said honestly. "I *would* like to marry you."

Hannah's mouth opened in shock, forming a perfect spot to kiss. "You do?" she said. It took all the will power he had to keep from drawing her into his arm and tasting those lips.

"We *must* marry." His words surprised him. It wasn't what he had meant to say and Hannah immediately misunderstood. Her cheeks paled and her eyes hardened.

"That's real gentlemanly of you, but you mustn't worry about my reputation, Mr. Savage, I never do. I understand about frontier gossip, and I always just rise above it."

"Maybe I'm thinking of my own reputation," Josh said, with a tiny smile. "I can't let folks around here label me a rounder. I've decided to settle right here in Guthrie. I like this country. I like it a lot." He held her gaze, hoping that his eyes spoke the words that seemed too hard for him to articulate.

Hannah's mouth fell open again. Josh felt his jaw twitch as he struggled to control a grin. He couldn't look at her without grinning like an idiot. He loved to tease her and make her smile. Sparring with Hannah Smith was more fun than anything he'd ever done. Not since he was a boy and exchanged banter with Ma had he known a woman who was as smart as he was. Smarter probably. And he knew, without a doubt, that he wanted, that he needed this woman.

Hannah shut her mouth and scowled. "Are you mocking me?" she asked.

"No, ma'am. What I'm trying to do is to court you. But I fear that I'm awkward as a newborn colt. Perhaps because I have no experience and need a bit of coaching?" This time he allowed himself a wide smile, sending up a short prayer that the words would soften the anger on her face.

Hannah just stared. He kept grinning, delighted that she didn't walk back into the kitchen and slam the door.

"And why would you do that?" she finally said. "It's not as if I'm the kind of woman who attracts men. I know very well that I'm both plain and dull." She looked at him defiantly.

It was Josh's turn to stare back in disbelief. It took a minute for him to recover from the shock of what he'd heard.

"Hannah Smith," he said honestly. "Where did you get such an idea? You're the prettiest and the most fascinating woman I've never met. If I could have dreamed up a wife it would have been you. Maybe those Kansans weren't smart enough to marry up with you, but don't hold their stupidity against me."

Hannah swallowed hard and then wet her lips. She studied his face as if for signs of teasing. Surely she could see that he was dead serious. Surely she knew him well enough to realize that he'd never tease anyone in such a cruel way. She swallowed again as if trying to find her voice.

"Well," she breathed softly, "For a man with no experience, I'd say you're doing right well for yourself." She smiled shyly at him.

Her smile punched him in the gut. "Hannah, I've got to tell you something about myself."

"And I want to hear." She looked at him the way he'd always wanted a woman to look at him.

Horses' hooves and wagon wheels sounded. Turley must have decided to bring the body back here. *But why?*

"Mr. Turley is coming back," Hannah said looking toward the road. "I wonder why he changed his mind about going into town?"

Josh's heart almost stopped. The U.S. Marshal was riding along beside the wagon, and he hadn't yet told Hannah that he worked for the U.S. Secret Service, or that he had come to her farm on purpose to arrest her husband.

***

Hannah surmised that the marshal must have been on the road riding in this direction and had met Turley. She calculated the amount of food prepared and decided that there were plenty of victuals for everyone. That lawman looked as if he could use a good meal.

Mr. Turley left the wagon at the turn-off to the road and began unhitching the mule while the marshal rode up to the house on his horse.

"Howdy folks." He tipped his hat. "I decided to ride out this way to check on Mrs. Smith." He nodded toward Josh. "Turley told me that you got shot up. He's leaving the shooter's carcass away from the house and downwind. Glad to see that you nailed both of your counterfeiters."

"Both? Counterfeiters?" Hannah gasped. "Whatever are you talking about?"

The marshal looked at her and then over at Josh. "Sorry, Savage, I figured you had already explained just who you are and what you're doing here."

Shock weighted Hannah's chest as if her heart had turned into an anvil. She had been a fool! She'd allowed *another* man to dupe her. A sort of numbness spread through her. A body couldn't trust any man, she thought. No man at all. She scowled at Josh, knowing that all of her disappointment and hurt showed plainly on her face.

"No. He has not explained anything." She pinned her gaze to his, forcing herself to show as little emotion as possible.

"Hannah..." Josh's voice was husky and his eyes pleaded for forgiveness, but Hannah steeled her heart against him. "I was just about to tell you."

"You lied to me," she said. "I thought you were some kind of lay preacher traveling through to Texas."

"And you believed that?" Mrs. Turley had stepped out to see who rode in. She turned to look up at her husband just striding up to the house, grinning broadly and rubbing his hands to warm them.

"Well, what's everyone doing standing out in the cold?" Turley said. "I say we wash up and then eat that Thanksgiving dinner the ladies have been working so hard on." Dead silence stopped him and he looked around in puzzlement. "Did I say something wrong? That fella in the wagon ain't going to care if he don't get buried for another few hours. He won't even stink that much worse."

Mrs. Turley stepped forward. "Well, you're right about that, and he's not likely to bother us neither since you've parked him away from the house. You men step to the pump and wash up while I dish up this good food. We got us two kinds of meat—rabbit and ham—I'd say that's right fancy for this special day." She turned toward the door and then looked back at Hannah.

"Miz Smith, I think you and Mr. Savage might have something to discuss before you come inside. We'll give you five minutes and then we're starting. We got us a lot to be thankful for today." She fixed Hannah with a hard look. "Iffen we don't let our own foolish pride keep us from the little bit of happiness that God tosses in our direction." She whirled her ample form around and bustled into the house.

Turley and the marshal headed to the pump and Josh shot a pleading glance at Hannah.

"We have to get out of this cold and talk. Let's go into the barn while I explain everything to you."

"And be attacked by that evil rooster? I think not. And I'll not spoil everyone else's Thanksgiving dinner by making them wait until the food is cold. You and I will go inside and be civil and polite to each other. Then I think you'll be well enough to ride the mile into town in the wagon. You should feel right at home with the stink." She whirled on her heel and almost ran inside. Instantly she regretted her words and her action. Why hadn't she given him a chance to explain? Why hadn't she listened to Mrs. Turley?

Feeling totally miserable, Hannah helped dish up the food. The marshal and Turley sat down with the look of hungry men, concerned only with having a good dinner. Mrs. Turley joined them and finally Hannah and Josh sat in the two remaining chairs—which happened to be side-by-side.

***

Josh hardly tasted the meal. How could he fix things with Hannah? It pained him that he had hurt her feelings. Was that rabbit or ham that he put in his mouth? He really didn't care. Finally Turley pushed away his plate and patted his belly.

"Best dinner I ever et," he said. "It'll be hard to find room for pie and a slice of cake, but I sure intend to try." The marshal murmured agreement and added his praise for the quality of the food.

Josh was tired of pretenses. He'd never been one to walk around a problem, no matter how difficult or embarrassing, and he wouldn't now. He pushed back his chair and stood, stopping the women from rising to fetch dessert.

"I have a few words to say to Hannah first." He'd stood too fast and pain from his wound shot through him. He sat down again and took her hand in his. "I've been wanting to explain who I am and what I'm about for the last few days, but was too much of a coward to get the job done. I had hoped for a little privacy for this task, but time has run out so I have no choice but to do it in front of God and everybody."

Astonishment and something else warred on Harriet's face. Did he see fear or hope? Or perhaps a combination of both? For once she seemed too stunned to speak, and for that he was grateful.

"For the last seven years I've been a Secret Service Field Agent investigating counterfeiting activities." Hannah sucked in her breath and pressed her hand against her heart. He hurried on to keep from having her interrupt.

"The trail of two counterfeiters brought me to Guthrie. I'd just ridden into town when you drove into town with your husband's body."

"My husband was a counterfeiter." she said sadly. "I can't believe that I married a criminal."

"You knew nothing about his crime," Josh said. "You were a bride who followed her husband to the Land Run."

"I knew in my heart that I shouldn't marry him, but I…"

"You had no choice," Josh finished the sentence for her. "I know that. But Smith was one of the men I hunted. I also wanted his partner. Most of all I wanted the plates they used to print bad money." He turned and looked at the marshal. "The two had a falling out near Kansas City. Smith bashed his partner, Gus Craven, over the head, leaving him for dead. Then he headed to the Territory thinking he'd be safe. But Craven recovered and followed Smith here."

"Well of all things," Mrs. Turley said. Her husband silenced her with a shake of his head. Josh continued speaking.

"I came here knowing that Craven would follow the plates and I intended to arrest both men and take the plates in to the authorities." He paused for a minute and turned to face Hannah. "What I didn't plan on was meeting you."

Josh swallowed hard wishing the others at the table would have the decency to walk outside and give him some privacy. But no one moved. Out of the corner of his eye he caught their different reactions: Mrs. Turley was smiling with her hand pressed to her heart. Her husband watched looking as if he wished the talking was over and he could get back to the important business of eating pie. The marshal mopped up gravy with one of Hannah's light-as-air dinner rolls. What the hell? Josh thought and focused on Hannah.

"I had a plan mapped out for my life. I was going to buy a cattle spread down in Texas with the money I'd saved. Never for a minute did I ever figure on being a farmer." He swallowed, and lowered his voice. "But there's no way I can ride out of here. Not and leave you behind. I want to marry you, Hannah."

Chapter Nine

Hannah finally found her voice. "Oh Josh, I don't want you giving up your dream in order to make mine come true."

He leaned forward and kissed her gently on the lips. "Your dream has become mine, Hannah. Staying in Guthrie is what I want."

Mrs. Turley murmured, "Ohhhhh." Hannah saw the sweet faced woman blot a tear with a well-worn handkerchief. Josh said he loved her! He had proposed—in front of three witnesses, no less—if this were a dream she didn't want to wake up. Ever.

"Yes. Oh yes," she said, still tingling from his kiss.

Josh pulled her to her feet and kissed her in a way she had never imagined, and which she was not at all sure was decent. His lips took possession of hers—first loving and gentle—then demanding and probing. The kiss thrilled her clear to her best high-button shoes. Everyone else at the table seemed to disappear. She was aware only of Josh's kiss and the feel of his arms around her, pressing her close to him.

Then she remembered his injury.

"Holding me is bound to hurt you," she said.

"More than you'll ever know," Josh said with a grin, and then kissed her again.

A loud clearing of the marshal's throat interrupted them. "Let me be the first to congratulate both of you. But right now I think that maybe we should hunt for those counterfeit plates. You have any idea where they might be hidden, Mrs. ...er, ma'am?"

Hannah struggled to regain her senses. The marshal hadn't wanted to call her, "Mrs. Smith," and that sent a ripple of pleasure through her. She didn't want him to call her that, either. Was it possible that folks might soon be calling her, Mrs. Savage? The thought made her heart swell with pride. Then she realized the marshal had repeated his question.

"Everyone here at this table is welcome to call me, Hannah," she said. "I don't know where those counterfeit plates might be," she said, remembering that she herself had hidden her divided riding skirt under the potatoes and covered it with straw. "But it shouldn't take too long to search this place."

The excitement of the hunt seemed more exciting to the group even than freshly baked pies, and soon everyone joined in the search. The marshal and Turley headed to the barn, Mrs. Turley to the root cellar, and Hannah was to check the henhouse. Everyone agreed that Josh should have the easier job of searching the house, because of his wound.

"I'll check the privy, first," Hannah said, glad to have a reason to make a needed stop. And she did riffle through the pages of cut newspapers stacked there. Then she went to the henhouse. Henry spotted her from his place in the yard and ran toward her with his wings flapping. Hannah raised the broom she carried.

"I'll not hesitate to whack you a good one," she said in a no-nonsense voice. Henry stopped a yard away from her and glared as he continued to flap his wings.

"You and I will never be friends," Hannah said. "But you once saved my life and my virtue, so let's us make a bargain. You keep away from me and I promise not to make dinner out of either you or one of your laying hens."

Henry stopped and cocked his head to one side. Then he flapped his wings again and made rooster-noises that worried Hannah. But he stayed a good yard away.

"All right then," Hannah said and walked inside his domain to look for plates. She scanned the small area: perches for the fowls, enameled watering trough, beat-up oyster shell pan and a few specks of grain that the hens had left from their morning feeding. There were no spots where there'd been any recent digging. Hannah made a mental note that she needed to shovel out the place in a couple of days, then she went back into the house.

Josh stood at the table grinning.

"You found the plates," she said.

"Nope, but I found something else mighty interesting." He held up her divided skirt.

Hannah smiled back. "George told me to burn that skirt," she said. "You might as well know that I bought it with my own money, and I intend to keep it and to wear it."

"I'm mighty glad to hear that," Josh said. "In a few more days I thought we might go riding together."

***

Half an hour later the group once again sat around the table eating dessert. The marshal looked up from his mince meat pie and spoke. "Smith must have buried it. It could take a man years to dig around this farm looking for those plates. You suppose he left a map anywhere?"

Josh shook his head. "I looked for such a thing when I searched the house. And believe me, I didn't miss anything." He shot a mischievous smile at Hannah. "Guess I'll have to spend the rest of my life digging up this place."

Hannah smiled back, figuring she looked silly as a young miss and not caring one whit. The marshal decided to try a slice of apple pie and Hannah automatically rose to cut him a bit of cheese she'd made. She was happier than she'd been in her whole life.

Her mind shot to the first evening she'd set foot on this homestead and how heart-sick she'd felt. George had strutted around like a bantam rooster, making her dread the thought of spending her life with him. And that freshly dug grave had worried her so. She'd thought George might have killed an innocent person. She stopped and clasped her hand to her heart.

"Oh my goodness! That's it!"

"What's it?" asked Josh.

"The grave! That must be where George buried the counterfeit plates! He said he'd killed a claim jumper, but I'd felt then that he was lying. George just wanted a place that he wouldn't forget and that no one would want to look in."

"Well, I'll be," Mrs. Turley said. "He were smarter than I figured he was."

Chapter Ten

After chores the next morning Hannah put on her white shirtwaist and the divided skirt and rode Josh's horse into town. It had been almost dark by the time the marshal tied his own horse to the wagon and left with the dead body and the counterfeit plates. Josh rode into town with him insisting that a mile in a wagon wouldn't hurt him. He planned to spend the night at the Grand Hotel and announced they'd be married the next morning.

Hannah boldly decided to ride astraddle, knowing that such an act would shock most townsfolk. Probably the men would be more outraged than the women. Men were frightened of change it seemed to Hannah, especially change that gave women any semblance of equal rights. She'd read angry editorials attacking women's suffrage in the newspapers that told of marches taking place back East. But women *would* get the vote, Hannah decided. Sooner or later such a day was coming. She just hoped it was during her lifetime.

Josh's horse was well trained and Hannah was both surprised and relieved at how easily he handled. The ride was pleasant until her unruly thoughts began to torment her. What if Josh had changed his mind overnight? What if she couldn't make him happy? Would riding into town wearing her brazen divided skirt embarrass him? She forced these thought out of her mind.

This wedding would be much happier than that first miserable ceremony. It would be a simple affair—a preacher marrying them somewhere convenient—and there would be no ring, but that wasn't important she told herself. She'd brought along her best dress to change into. Her blue wool. It wasn't fancy, but it would do just fine. A ring and a new dress weren't that important. What was important was that Josh loved her. He *loved* her!

A sudden shyness struck her as she rode down Main Street. Her cheeks grew hot as every eye seemed to turn in her direction. Why on earth had she ridden astraddle? She could just as easily have turned to the side when she reached town.

Just then she spotted a group of men standing in the middle of the brick street. Each was dressed in his Sunday best and each wore a big smile. Josh stood inches above the others and held the biggest bouquet of hothouse flowers she'd ever seen. Along side him was a man she didn't know who held a Bible. Mr. Turley and the marshal completed the gathering. She rode to within five feet of them and reined in her horse. What on earth was going on?

Josh strode to Hannah, helped her dismount and then placed the flowers in her arms. "I'm holding you to your promise to marry me," he said. "I even have the preacher here with me. Everything is ready and planned. We're to be married in the Grand Hotel just down the street, and then spend the night. Turley here said he'd look after our livestock."

"I've brought my blue wool dress to wear," Hannah said shyly. "Might I change clothes in the hotel?"

"You look mighty pretty in that fancy skirt," Josh said. "But I wanted you to have something new to start out our life in. I bought a real fine dress at one of the local stores and I have a dressmaker ready to alter it, if need be. Miss Radine at the Grand Hotel has a room ready for you to bathe and dress in. Then after the wedding we'll stay in their bridal suite."

"Oh my goodness," Hannah said. Was this a dream? Would she wake up and find herself on a scratchy straw tick. "Oh my goodness."

"Would you feel cheated if I asked you to wear my mother's wedding ring? If you want a new one, I'll buy which ever you choose, but I'd really like you to wear Ma's ring. I've carried her ring and her Bible with me everywhere I've gone. It's mighty precious to me—and so are you.

"Oh, yes! Yes, yes, yes."

Josh's hand touched her back and sent shivers down her spine. He gently guided her toward the wooden sidewalk.

"Sweetheart," he said, "I'm looking forward to a long life with you. I'm thinking that there will never be a dull moment.

"I expect not," Hannah said.

"I plan to buy you a wedding present," Josh said. "Pick out anything your heart desires."

Hannah thought for a minute and then smiled.

"I'd like a bolt of yellow gingham for curtains and a pound of coffee to keep on hand to be sure I never run out."

The Best of Christmas Flowers

Peggy Fielding

Peggy Moss Fielding is a native Okie who lives in Tulsa, Oklahoma. She is a full time writer with a great many books, articles and short stories to her credit. She has lived in Japan, Cuba and the Republic of the Philippines. Her most recent full length novel is titled *Scoundrels' Bargain*.

Chapter 1

Drumright, Oklahoma~September 1916

When she heard a tiny sound from the woods, eleven year old Lily placed her book on the bench in front of her. It was still light enough to read but it was time for Pansy to be coming home and she didn't want to miss a moment of that. Her sister looked up from her own reading.

"Daisy, run on inside. Give me your book." The younger girl sighed and handed her book to Lily. "Go on in now, hon, and wash up before bed." She caught the edge of Daisy's apron. "Don't sit on the bed until Mama folds down the counterpane." She whispered the next words to her young sister. "You know how Mama is, honey."

When the screen door slammed behind her younger sister, Lily moved to sit on the wooden bench. She didn't want to miss a thing. When her older sister had left for school she'd been wearing her green flowered cotton dress that Lily had tried to make somewhat like a fashionable hobble skirt. She checked the drape of the skirt early on, just after the two of them had washed the family's breakfast dishes.

Pansy always looks good on her horse, Lily thought, but the green dress she had sewn to look like the smartest hobble skirt, even though it had a split skirt, looked especially good when Pansy was riding the feisty roan. Papa always bought a race horse for Pansy if he could find one. She loved to ride fast.

It had been such fun for the two of them when Papa had given them money to shop for three dress lengths after Pansy was accepted at the convent business school. They'd chosen the green–flowered print, a blue–striped twill and a dark brown and black plaid crash. Pansy also wore her gray silk Sunday dress for special days at the business school, usually for the nun's holiday celebrations in their church.

Lily shook her head at the thought. Four dresses! Think of that. Pansy sure deserved them. She was the smartest of all the Flowers and she could ride better than anyone. And now! Now she was an *Eighth Grade Graduate*, not to mention that she was enrolled in business school. Her trip home today promised to be especially exciting, really romantic. Pansy had told her, over the dishes, "I'll be coming home in a surrey with fringe on the top."

"With a boy?"

"Uh–huh. A boy from school. He asked me yesterday if he could bring me home."

"What about Rosey?"

"Oh, we'll just tie her to the back. She won't mind."

Lily leaned closer to the banister. She didn't want to miss a thing! Pansy always had such romantic adventures.

"I can't wait until it's my turn to ride in a buggy with a boy," Lily murmured.

She straightened. Pansy and the boy were coming down the trail that Papa had blazed for the family when they'd first moved to Drumright. She could hear the jingle of the harness, the plodding of the horses' hooves.

And that wasn't all! The boy driving the surrey was singing and playing some kind of instrument, maybe a ukulele? Lily could hardly believe her ears. This was the most exciting thing she had ever heard, if only such a romantic adventure could also be hers when she graduated from eighth grade.

Three years. She promised herself. Three years and maybe she too could have it all, the boy, the songs, the buggy and a big moon rising.

"Pansy is so lucky," Lily whispered. "I can't wait until I'm fourteen." She stood to be ready to take Rosie to the barn so Pansy could have a chance to say "good night" to the boy without a younger sister hanging around.

In a couple of years it would be her turn to ride in a surrey with a boy who could sing, "There's a Long, Long Trail A-Winding."

She had a boyfriend at school. Sometimes Tom Moss would put his hand on her shoulder at recess time. She'd been told that Tom could sing, that all the other Moss boys could sing.

She'd been told more than once that she couldn't carry a tune but she knew the words of the song. She mouthed the words along with Pansy's friend.

> There's a long, long trail a-winding
> Into the land of my dreams,
> Where the nightingales are singing
> And a white moon beams:

There's a long, long night of waiting
Until my dreams all come true;
Till the day when I'll be going down
That long, long trail with you

Chapter 2

"I've got news," Pansy whispered across Rosie's saddle while she and Lily prepared to rub down the animal.

"Oh, what?" Lily couldn't wait to hear. Her big sister led such an exciting life. "Tell me what's happened."

Her sister smiled. "I'm going to tell *everyone* at the supper table. You'll hear then, Lily."

"Let's hurry then, and get everything on the table." Lily hung the curry comb on the outside of Rosie's stall. The two sisters giggled and whispered on their walk toward the kitchen.

"Did you tell Papa that a boy was bringing you home in a buggy last night?"

"No, guess I forgot."

"Oh, Pansy, I can't believe you didn't ask permission."

"Well Lily girl, everyone in or near Drumright, Oklahoma, knows that Blackie Flowers can outfight, out-ride, out-work, out-yell and out-shoot any male citizen of this area or maybe anyone in the whole state. No boy would *dare* to get fresh with one of Blackie Flowers' daughters." She put an arm around Lily's shoulders. "So since you're one of Blackie Flowers' daughters also, that means they won't try any funny stuff with you either, Lil."

"I haven't been out with any boys."

"Won't be long until they'll be flocking around you girl, pretty as you are. And you can be sure they'll be *quite* respectful." Pansy grinned down at Lily and her gray eyes sparkled. "We can thank Papa for that."

"No boy has asked to take me out, yet." Lily opened the door, gesturing to Pansy to step in ahead of her.

"Your time is coming, Lil. I promise."

"I can't wait to hear the secret you're going to share at the table." Lily took a deep breath, "Oh my. Does Mama know about it? She's already started chicken to frying. I guess she knows this is going to be a special supper?"

"I didn't tell her." Pansy shrugged. "But you know how Mama is. She knows things. Let's wash up and get the table set. Papa is going to come riding in any minute."

"Yeah, and he'll be hungry as a bear!"

After Mama had invited Violet to say Grace, and Papa had shouted his usual hearty "Amen," the six of them dug into the mashed potatoes, gravy, squash, green beans and fried chicken.

Lily took the two wings, the pieces of the chicken that had been "assigned" to her when she was even younger than Daisy was now.

As her mother scooped the heart, liver and gizzard onto her own plate she smiled at Lily. Lily had often heard Mama say, "The cook always gets the heart."

Good eating probably, Lily thought, but not much meat for a hardworking cook. Sometimes Mama also took the neck when she took the giblets.

Lily knew that some Drumright folks served baked turkey for Thanksgiving and Christmas but her family always looked forward to fried chicken, especially when they'd had Brother Lackey or even relatives as guests. Lily had heard tell that Baptist preachers were famous for loving fried chicken. Whenever Brother Lackey came to eat with the Flowers family, he was always given first choice from the platter of chicken. Mama usually tried to offer two chickens when the preacher was coming. But tonight was just family.

Before Daisy and Violet cleared the table Mama nodded to Pansy and smiled. Now they'd get to hear the big news.

"Pansy Lou," Mama smiled at Papa, then at Pansy, "Now hon, you wanted to tell all of us something really important?"

"Yes ma'am. Of course you all know I graduated from business school last Friday?" Everyone, including Mama and Papa nodded in concert.

Lily had to grin. Pansy always knew how to get everybody's attention. Papa sometimes called his older daughter his "drama queen."

He sometimes called Lily his "good girl."

Lily considered the difference in the two titles. Maybe it would be more exciting to be a "drama queen," but it wasn't bad to be known as "Blackie's Good Girl."

"Well," Pansy poured thick cream onto the blackberry cobbler on her plate, before she took a bite. "I've found myself a job."

Gasps rose and all eyes focused on the oldest daughter.

"What kind of job?" Daisy's question echoed the thoughts of everyone else at the table, Lily realized.

"I'll be working at the produce house, starting next week."

"What'll you be doing girl?" That was Blackie. "Not plucking chickens, I hope."

"Oh no, Papa, I'll be keeping books in the office for the produce house and for their little grocery store."

"Yay!" That came from Daisy. "My big sister is famous!"

"And rich!" That was Violet's shout.

"Well, not rich, but along with my salary, I will get an employee discount on anything we might want to buy from the produce house or grocery."

"What can we get from the prudoe house?" Daisy asked.

"That's *produce house*, honey." Mama smoothed Daisy's two long braids. "We could get grain and other good stuff that might be useful to our family."

"What kind of stuff?"

"Well, flour or cornmeal. Sometimes special fruit or vegetables for instance."

Daisy nodded.

"Or even baby chickens," Pansy offered.

Both younger sisters whooped and applauded for Pansy's employee discount, especially for the baby chickens.

"Good job, Pansy." Mama touched the shoulder of her oldest. "We're so proud of you."

"Papa, after we get the table cleared could you bring out your fiddle?" Violet pleaded. "We can all sing." She cheered at her Father's nod and she and Daisy rushed into their regular chore of clearing and cleaning the table.

Lily felt as pleased as the little girls because singing with Papa was almost as much fun as "Reading Nights" when Mama read aloud from one of the books Lily brought from school. *Almost.*

Girl of the Limberlost had been so exciting last week.

Chapter 4
May 1918

"Well, so you're graduated from eighth grade. You going to business school at the convent, the way your big sister did?"

Lily looked up at Dom, Pansy's new boyfriend, the man she'd met at the produce house. Lily was so short she found most men to be tall, but this guy, this Dom Tucci, was really, really tall. And big—broad shouldered, blonde, extremely handsome, for sure. She couldn't blame Pansy for being so crazy about the man. His Louisiana accent had the effect of warm syrup on buttered pancakes.

When he came out to their house he made the living room feel crowded, somehow uncomfortable, Lily thought.

Pansy had been thrilled when Dom had quit his job at the produce house to take a job on the Drumright Police Force.

"Oh, no, Dom, Papa has told me I have to stay in school. He says I don't have the head for business that Pansy has. He thinks a high school diploma will help me, that I might be able to teach."

The man's light blue gaze shifted to her body. Lily stepped back a bit. All the Flowers, even Papa, loved the guy, but he scared Lily just a little.

"I'm not as smart as Pansy. Papa thinks more schooling is 'specially important for me."

"Your Dad tells you you're not smart?"

"Well, I'm not as smart as my sister but Papa always calls me his 'good girl,' so that's a compliment, isn't it?"

"I'm crazy about Pansy, hon, but I've always thought you were prettier. No wonder the boys are coming around these days."

Lily had to laugh. "Yeah, the Moss brothers seem to like me."

"I mean it, little girl. That black as a crow's wings hair, those huge blue eyes, and your porcelain skin. Not to mention your great figure, tiny waist and all. Lily girl, you're what they used to call a 'pocket Venus'."

"Yeah," Lily stared up, up, up, at the southerner who was even taller than Blackie Flowers, the largest man in town, she'd always believed. "Pansy towers over me."

Violet burst in the front door, limping and leaning on Daisy, who was crying.

"A man hit Violet," Daisy screamed the words then resumed her loud crying.

"A man hit you?" The ice blue eyes of Pansy's boyfriend seemed to glare at the two little girls. His hand touched the holstered gun which hung at his hip. "Who was he? What did he hit you with?"

"His car," Daisy screamed through the tears she was shedding for her sister.

Dom squatted to look at Violet's knee. The left side of her leg was scraped and a tiny trickle of blood eased down her leg.

"Are you okay, Violet?"

She nodded "yes" to his question.

"Who was the guy?"

"Mr. Turner. He was in the car that he drives to church."

"Did he stop to look at your leg? Did he bring you home?"

Daisy continued to sob between her shouted words. "He didn't even stop, Dom."

Lily felt the blood drain from her face...not because of the tiny injury to her little sister's leg but because of the big, blonde man's reaction.

He stood, his pale blue eyes turned to ice, his hand leaped to touch his gun holster.

"Yeah, I know that old bastard." He stalked from the room without another word.

"Where's Dom going, Lily?"

"To find Mr. Turner, I think, honey. I hope he doesn't find him." Lily toyed with the idea of running through Drumright's back alleys to Mr. Turner's place, to warn him. No use, she realized, Dom was on his motorcycle. He'd be at the Turner's house in a few minutes.

She fell to her knees beside Violet. She closed her eyes in prayer. "God, please protect Mr. Turner," then she looked at the scraped leg. "No more crying Daisy. Come on Violet. Let's go to the kitchen and I'll doctor you up."

"No iodine!" Violet screamed.

"No iodine," Lily promised. "I'll just clean it and put a dab of Mama's calendula salve on you." She took the hands of each of her sisters and led them toward the pump in the kitchen. "I'll try not to hurt you."

After supper Dom returned to report Mr. Turner to be properly penitent. "Said he didn't realize he'd even hit the kid."

Pansy's gray eyes held a bit of trepidation, Lily thought, when her older sister asked, "Did you do anything bad to that old man, Dom?"

"Oh, banged him a bit, didn't really hurt him. Reckon he'll drive a little more careful now."

He looked down the table at the two smallest sisters. "You two kids stay on the sidewalks. Don't step out into the street unless some big person is with you. You hear me?"

The two girls nodded and Lily saw smiles all around the table. I must be the only one worried about Mr. Turner, she thought.

Blackie lifted his glass of sweet cider towards the blonde policeman. "Thanks for taking such good care of my girls." Mama nodded her agreement.

Lily felt a chill sweep through her, even though it wasn't cold in the room.

Pansy's proud smile sparkled toward the big blonde policeman who'd worn his holstered gun to the table, even though he'd removed his leather jacket and the leather hat that fastened under his chin. Lily always thought the goggles on his hat made him look even more menacing.

I'll visit Mr. and Mrs. Turner tomorrow, Lily silently promised herself. The two of them must be scared spitless.

Chapter 5
December 31, 1919

Lily counted how many Christmas holidays had passed since she'd been so envious of Pansy's romantic life, the homemade hobble skirt, her rides in surreys and buggies, her serenades from her escorts.

That had been long enough ago that she'd seen skirts shortened, surreys warehoused in farmers' barns or trashed somehow in favor of model T's or other automobiles.

By now she'd had plenty of dates, mostly with the Moss boys, (other than the youngest boy, Hoss, or the shyest brother, Red). She'd walked and ridden with the four other brothers but not a one of them had played an instrument or sung a song to her. Certainly, none of them had quoted poetry for her. They were always very respectful in their behavior, however.

"Well," she murmured, "That's progress, I suppose. Romance such as your big sister used to have is out the window for you, Miss Lily."

At that moment Pansy came from their bedroom to stand near Lily. She leaned to whisper in Lily's ear.

"Sister, I want you to stay with me today. No matter what happens, stay right with me. Will you do that? Will you stick right with me?"

Lily nodded. "I'll stay with you Pansy." She felt a bit frightened at the need for the promise, and puzzled by Pansy's request. Was Pansy afraid of something? Of *someone*? Did she think Lily would be able to defend her against some sort of trouble?

"I mean it, sis. I want you to stay right beside me all day. Right with me until we go to our bed."

Again Lily nodded. She took Pansy's hand. "I did tell Bundy Moss I'd go out for ice cream this afternoon."

"Ice cream?" Pansy smiled. "It's near freezing today and you're going out for ice cream?"

Chapter 6

January 1, 1920

Lily had never even noticed when Pansy slipped from their featherbed. She must have been extremely quiet because none of the rest of the family had been aware that the oldest daughter had gone from the house without a word.

"She didn't even leave a note?" Lily asked.

"No." Blackie Flowers' answer betrayed his shock. "But she went willingly, I guess." He took Mama's hand into his own. "Up the road I found her shoeprints on one side of the prints of the motorcycle tires. *His* were on the other side. He'd walked the machine in. Then they walked the cycle out. They'd planned the whole thing, I guess." His voice trembled slightly. "You'd think they could have said *something*. We wouldn't have stood in her way. All of us liked the boy."

Mama nodded.

Except me, Lily thought, Dom scared me. She felt her heart well with sadness. That's why Pansy wouldn't let me out of her sight yesterday. She knew she'd be leaving today. She didn't expect to see any of us ever again.

Before many more weeks had passed, the rest of the Flowers family had also come to Lily's silent *understanding*. Their beautiful and smart Pansy Lou was gone for good.

Blackie gave them the bad news one night at the table. "I went to the police station today. Jack Ary says Dom quit a few days before they disappeared. He told Ary he was going back to Louisiana."

"Where in Louisiana?" Mama asked. "Did the chief say which town?"

"Ary didn't know." Blackie rubbed his hand across his face in a gesture of frustration. "Just Louisiana is all the boy told him."

"Papa, I don't think Dom is a boy. He looks like a man grown, to me." Anger shook Lily's inner being. "I think he's almost ten years older than Pansy. She's a girl and he's a man who persuaded her to go off with him. He took our Pansy away from us."

Her father nodded, made another tired swipe across his face then headed for the door.

"You kids go on to school now," he ordered. "I want every one of you girls to finish high school." He turned to look at Lily's mother. "You see they get to school, hon. They'll be safer there than anywhere."

"Where are you going?" Mama's voice held surprise. "I thought you were going to plow today."

"I am, but I'm going to the police station to talk to Chief Jack Ary first. Maybe he'll remember something."

Chapter 8
July 1920

"Is that a motorcycle?" Bundy Moss pushed his chair back from the table and strode to the front door. He easily beat the Flowers family.

"Pansy," he shouted over his shoulder and yanked the entry door open for the oldest Flowers daughter. He stepped out the door and closed it firmly behind himself.

"You bastard." He crouched slightly and pulled a small handgun from his boot.

Dom stripped off his leather cap and jacket and threw them into the cycle's sidecar.

"Who the hell are you?"

"A friend of Lily Flowers, as if you didn't know."

"I don't remember you, boy."

"Tucci, you bastard. You've sold me many a pint from that sidecar. You know who I am...Bundy Moss. I'm tempted to shoot you for what you've done to this little family."

Dom raised both hands. "I married the damned girl, Moss. They won't be so upset about that. They expected it, I think."

"Where'd you take her?" Bun lowered the gun slightly.

"Oh, we spent most of the time down in Krebs."

"No oil down there. It's just a spot in the road."

"Yeah, I'm not in the oil business. There's a café. A few friends. A church."

Lily slipped through the front door and stepped out to stand at Bun's shoulder.

"Bun put that gun away. They're married and she's going to have a baby. All is well." She touched Bundy's arm. "Come on in, you two big roosters. Mama says we need to come to the table."

The two men followed her back into the house; Bun following Dom as if keeping an eye on him.

Chapter 9
December 25, 1921

Lily wished she could feel as happy about Dom becoming a member of the family. He was going back into Jack Ary's force and he apparently had pretty grandiose plans for himself and for her sister.

"It can't hurt to let my smart little wife run all the Tucci enterprises while I spend my days rounding up bad guys. We just might get rich." The big, blonde man snorted with laughter. "We made some good contacts while we were hanging around down in Krebs, getting married and all that stuff."

The hair rose on the backs of Lily's arms. What kind of contacts was he talking about? What was this Krebs place he was talking about? She decided to ask Pansy to tell her everything. Oh, she took a deep breath. Easier said than done, of course, now, Pansy would not be sharing her bed. She wasn't even sharing the Flowers' house.

Pansy would be living with her husband and sharing his bed. It would be hard to whisper secrets when they were only seeing each other upon occasion.

Maybe she could ask Bun. He knew a lot of unusual things and the men in the oil field gossiped more than any group of women. He'd told her that, but he'd refused to pass on any scandalous stories. "I like it that you're an innocent kid," he'd said.

When the Christmas dinner was over, Lily walked to the drug store with Bun. Over ice cream, Lily listened to Bun's surprising explanation of Krebs.

"A bunch of bad guys from all over, mostly Eyetalians, show up there whenever the heat's on. After all, which G–man or Fed is gonna expect a bunch of Mafia hitmen are going to be huddled up in a little country town in the middle of Oklahoma. Krebs keeps itself pretty quiet."

"Mafia? What's that? Something bad?"

"Yeah, that's a name that Eyetalian gangsters call themselves. Prohibition will give them guys a whole new job. You know what a bootlegger does, Lily?"

"Sells whiskey?"

"Yeah, the guy brings it right to your door, or you show up at his place. All you have to do is pay the guy and tell him what you want next time."

"But it's against the law to sell alcohol in Oklahoma, isn't it? Has been since it was Indian Territory."

"Yeah, them Southern Mafia guys love it that Oklahoma is stuffed full of Baptists."

"Baptists? We're Baptist." Lily frowned at her friend.

"Yeah." Bun grinned down at her.

"What do you mean about the Baptists?"

"Both groups want liquor to be against the law."

"Well, Bun, what were Pansy and Dom doing in a place like that?"

"I suspect Southern Mafia connection, hon. I guess that tells you something about that big, blonde giant who married your sis, doesn't it?"

"Oh! *He's* Mafia?"

"Well, hon, what do you think they were doing in Krebs?"

"I don't know Bun. What do you think?"

"The guy hasn't had a job for six months. He has been hanging around in a town a sixteenth the size of Drumright but he comes back to his job as policeman and he's buying a big house. They've been saying around town that he and Pansy have ordered a great big green Buick. Where'd they get that kind of money, my sweet Lily?"

Lily put her hands over ears and shook her head. "I don't want to hear any more."

"You asked!"

"Please Bun. My family loves him!"

"Yeah. I know."

"And Pansy is our family favorite!"

"Uh huh."

"Oh, let's got home." She took her last bite of vanilla ice cream. "Mama and I fried a ton of chicken for our Christmas dinner. I bet she'd give you some to take out on the job with you."

"Sounds good. Let's head back to the Flowers' Christmas garden."

Chapter 10

March 1922

"Mama, the doctor says he thinks I'm going to have twins. That's why I'm so huge."

Her mother clasped her hands together. "Two grandchildren." She reached for her oldest then turned to look at Lily. "I'll be a grandma and you, Lily, you'll be an Aunt, my girl. Two times. What do you think about that?"

Lily could hardly quell the scream of joy that rose inside her. Babies! Twins! She just couldn't wait These twins would be the best loved kids in the history of the world, with three adoring aunts, two idolizing grandparents and a smart, hard working mother to guide their steps.

"When will they be here, darling?" Mama looked as eager as Lily felt.

"Any day now, Mama," Pansy touched her jutting belly. "I feel like a cow. I'm so glad we have our new house pretty well cleaned up and painted." Pansy looked down at her nonexistent lap. "I guess we're going to have to turn it into a boarding house. Dom says we need to make a little money."

Oh what good news. Dom and Pansy were short of money. Discussion of a boarding house pleased Lily. Maybe they weren't using money from those Mafia people since they were trying to make a living on a policeman's salary and money made from renting rooms and cooking for strangers.

"It's going to be a lot of work, Mama. I sure would like to have Lily help me some, especially on Friday, Saturday and Sunday. People tell me that will be our busiest time and I'll need someone to help take care of the babies while I'm tending to business."

"Oh Mama. Could I?" Lily clasped her hands as if in prayer. "Taking care of the new babies would be so much fun."

"Oh, yes indeed, Lily. Violet and Daisy can do the chores around home. They're getting to be such helpful young ladies nowadays."

"Thanks Mama." Lily and Pansy spoke in concert. They grinned at each other, then hooked their little fingers together as they shouted, "Jinx, I owe you two wishes," just as they'd done when they were little kids. Now they just had to make their wishes.

You couldn't tell your wish, of course, but Lily felt she and Pansy might be wishing for the same thing...that she might come to the boarding house for three evenings a week to help with the babies. They still had to get Papa's permission.

"Dom's saying we're calling the boarding house 'Pansy's House.'" Pansy whispered. She didn't look too happy about the title.

Lily nodded and felt really proud of all that Pansy had accomplished. No question, her beautiful gray eyed older sister was a really smart woman and such a hard worker.

And it was time for her babies to join the Flowers' family even if they were Tucci's, Julia and Dom Tucci, Jr.

Chapter 11
November 1922

Lily couldn't believe the newborns, both the boy and the girl, had almost white hair. The little blondes were modeled on their father. Lily realized that Pansy was ecstatic about the little darlings' resemblance to Dom. They were big, beautiful healthy looking babies. Lily loved them madly.

The girl, Julia, often cried and screamed almost without ceasing. The boy, Junior, was the larger twin. He slept and ate as much as he was offered, and then he sometimes called out for more.

Lily had fallen in love with the two, whom she knew would become her special charges after Pansy had recovered and gotten back to work at the boarding house.

Now she'd be sleeping with them and feeding them and playing with them every weekend and probably at other times as well. Best news ever. She'd go straight to Pansy's house from Drumright High School after classes on Fridays. Christmas was coming up and they now had new babies, as well as Baby Jesus, to celebrate. Lily began plans for making something for Christmas for each member of her family.

Chapter 12
December 1924

It took a moment for Lily to rouse herself from deep sleep. She didn't need to look at the kids. She felt one on her right and one on her left. Sound asleep. What had wakened her?

Voices?

The bedroom door stood open. A tall man stood holding a lamp with the wick turned low. He stood with another much shorter man. Lily peered through her lashes. She didn't want to wake the children but what were these men doing?

"Hey, here's the one I want. Young, pretty, new to whoring. What's she doing with kids?"

"Those are Pansy's kids." The tall man holding the lamp whispered loudly enough that Lily could hear his words, "This is the sister that takes care of the kids while Pansy runs the business."

Oh. The men were probably checking in to the boarding house. Lily relaxed and continued to pretend sleep.

"Well, I want a drink," the short man whispered back. "Then I want this pretty little whore, but she'll need to get rid of the kids."

"Are you crazy?" The tall man's whisper was sharp on the air. "You can get that drink here. After all, Dom is a bootlegger, but this girl is no whore. This is Blackie Flowers' daughter. She's a good girl. He'd kill you if you ever touched her!"

"Isn't Pansy her sister?"

"Yeah. He'd kill you iffen you hurt her either, but I expect he *knows* she's running a whorehouse."

"Well, hell."

"Yeah. And Dom is someone to be scared of also. Old Blackie wouldn't hold a candle to Dom Tucci. He's a truly bad guy, for sure. Stay away from this girl." As he moved away she heard him add something about the Moss brothers.

Lily stiffened in the bed. They'd been discussing her, her father, her sister and her brother–in–law. Unbelievable!

She pulled her niece and nephew closer. She had to protect these children. She had to get out of this place. She had to talk to her big sister. She had to go home to speak to her father and mother, but first, she had to pray for the strength to bear all the horror which now engulfed her.

The click of the closing door seemed to tell her that she need not try to "straighten everything out" right now. That sleep would ready her for a very difficult day to come.

Her last thoughts before sleep, was that Christmas was almost here. She made a plan for crocheting warm hats for the children. The rest of her problems were now squarely in the hands of God.

Chapter 13
Mid-December 1924

When the children woke shouting hunger, Lily cleaned both of them and washed her own face and hands, after all were dressed she headed for the back stair that led down to the kitchen. The new cook would be frying bacon and eggs and making toast. That gas stove made cooking so easy.

Mama was still using a wood stove because, even though the Flowers were living close to Drumright, they hadn't yet been connected to the city gas line.

She froze on the middle step when the words "whorehouse" appeared in her mind.

"Can't be," Lily whispered into the cries of the hungry twins. "Pansy? Running a whorehouse? No, no." She took a hesitant step down. She could hear people talking in the kitchen. Another step down and she decided Dom was there because she heard shouting. Yeah, his voice. He sounded angry.

The shouting became louder with her next step. She looked down at the once again sleeping infants. I'd better take them back upstairs, she thought. They don't need to be involved in whatever is going on down there.

In the bedroom Lily took several pillows from the dresser drawers and the ones on the bed to make a nest for the sweet little blonde creatures. She packed them into the nest and covered them with a quilt that had been made by her mother. Her smile and her light kiss were benedictions on the youngsters she loved so much.

At the door she glanced at them once again. They seemed safe. One side of the bed was shoved against the south wall and the iron head board was against the west wall. The curly iron footboard protected them there. She could leave them for a minute or two, surely.

The noise from the kitchen increased and Lily raced to the back stairway once again. What was going on? She could hear Pansy and Dom and two of the boarders then the shouting moved out onto the back porch. No breakfast fragrance rose in the air. Had the cook caused some sort of quarrel? Or perhaps some of the boarders?

Pansy had asked her to stay in her room with the children as much as possible, to keep them entertained, fed and happy there, as much as possible. Someone, maybe the cook, came each day and picked up the slop jar from outside the room then returned it clean and ready for use.

When she took the twins for walks to visit their grandmother she placed them in the very fancy, woven rattan, double baby buggy which Pansy told her had come from Chicago. It was kept in the dining room because it was difficult to maneuver on the stairs. Sometimes Bun or Tom Moss helped her move the buggy, babies and all, down the front steps.

She'd often wondered what she would have done without the Moss boys' help. They all worked in the oil fields and all but the oldest lived with their parents just two blocks up the hill from 'Pansy's Place.' Lily always felt shock when she remembered that the Moss boys' father had served in the War Between the States. Such a long time ago, and the old man was still alive.

Where is a Moss when I need one?" She murmured as she tiptoed down the backstairs again. No need for quiet. The fracas on the back porch had only increased in sound. The boarders had on their nightclothes. Dom wore his leather motorcycle trousers and his white shirt.

She peered through the kitchen door. Some of the lady boarders seemed involved in the loud set-to. One of them, a plump redhead, screamed and fell to the floor.

"Dom!" That was Pansy's voice. "You coshed Clara. Why'd you do that? Have you killed the girl?"

"No, but I should have." The other lady boarders and the cook were all exclaiming and looking at redheaded Clara, either dead or unconscious on the floor of the porch. "She's been skimming on us, Pansy. We have to keep these girls in line."

He held the leather covered sand filled weapon up so all the women in the semicircle there could see it. "My favorite weapon. Easy to hide in my hand. No whore ever sees it coming." He put the cosh into his shirt pocket. "All you girls get the message?" He looked at each of the women in front of him, including Pansy. He stood with his broad shouldered back to Lily. Everyone was focused on the huge man. All of them nodded understanding, including Pansy.

Clara never stirred.

Bastard! Lily found herself thinking a word she had *never* used. Bastard!

Lily shifted her attention to the huge pot of water boiling for later washing and scalding the breakfast dishes.

Without another thought she grabbed the towels hanging from the stove's oven handles. She lifted the bale with her towel covered right hand, and held the pot bottom with her towel wrapped left. Water still at a rolling boil she took three steps and tossed all the scalding water directly onto the back of her brother-in-law.

He screamed and stumbled forward into the semicircle of women. Shouts of pain echoed while he ran and leaped from the porch as if to leave the burning pain behind him.

Drops of the water splashed on the unconscious Clara and she roused to a sitting position.

Pansy stared at Lily standing in the doorway still holding the empty pot. Her silver gaze held shock and question...her "good girl" sister had attacked the giant she was married to.

Dom had thrown himself against the neighbor's well cowling. He groaned and panted as he brought up the wooden bucket filled with water which he immediately lifted and poured over his back. His moan of relief spoke of the still blistering pain under his white shirt. He yanked the shirt from the waistband of his leather trousers.

Pansy raced to her husband to tear the shirt open and then try to be gentle as she removed the white cloth from his quivering body.

Lily saw her sister take the brown leather sap from the shirt pocket, then drop the weapon into the well. Dom continued making whimpering sounds while he tore at the front placket of his leather trousers. His behind must hurt too, even though he was wearing leather pants, she thought.

She wished she'd tossed the water towards his front rather than his back. This was the man who had made her wonderful sister into a whore mistress, a madam! She'd seen him almost kill a young woman, a prostitute who was working for him...and her sister.

Bitterness flooded Lily's mind. I wish I had killed the man, she thought, God help me, I want that man dead. A picture of the twins she adored rose behind her eyes. She wanted the death of her niece and nephew's father. She pictured them lying in the nest she'd made for them up stairs.

I'm taking them home to Mama and Papa, she decided. They'll be safe there. She raced back up the stairs, took a child in each arm and skittered back down to the dining room and the rattan double baby buggy.

She decided to say nothing about Dom, the scalding, the beaten whore...or Pansy, to Blackie or her Mama. No use killing them with all those horrid stories. She'd just say Pansy wanted the kids to stay with Mama and Blackie for a while.

Her parents would both love having their grandchildren to themselves for a few days. Good that it was a warm December. She'd just wheel the kids out to the street. Maybe one of the Moss boys would drive her home with the babies and their buggy. She struggled with the buggy to the street, then turned right toward the house where the Mosses lived.

Chapter 14
Almost Christmas 1924

The youngest Moss boy, Hoss, tucked the buggy into the rumble seat of his Chevrolet coupe and held the infants while Lily settled herself inside the old car, then Hoss handed the children in to her. They didn't cry while he cranked the engine to life. Both seemed to know they were being cared for.

After the car started, Hoss pulled a large peppermint stick from the pocket of his Yale High School athletic jacket.

"Oh, you graduated from high school over in Yale, Hoss?"

"Yeah, first high school grad among the Moss boys." He handed her the peppermint stick. "Bun told me you liked peppermint candy better than chocolate. This is his Christmas present for you."

"Oh thanks Hossy, and please thank Bun for me. You boys are all so nice to me."

"Where you going with the twins?"

"To Mama's place," Lily considered how much she should tell Hossy. "Blackie wants us to come and stay with them now."

He gave her a questioning look before he spoke. "I think you're smart to do that. We Mosses don't much like you staying at the Pansy Place, even on the weekends."

"I don't think I will stay there anymore."

"Good." He moved the stick shift and the small car rolled out into the road, heading towards the Flowers' acreage just at the edge of town.

The children slept soundly all the way to their grandparents' house.

Lily felt herself relax against the worn mohair upholstery. She and the twins were safe now, at least for the moment. What were Pansy and the others doing with Dom, she wondered. By now he had Doctor Starr with him, probably inside the "whorehouse" as Lily had now recognized "Pansy's Place" to be. The big oaf was probably lying face down in one of the rooms. What could Doctor Starr do with a man who had been scalded?

The picture of the big man's red back, strips of skin hanging from the white shirt when Pansy had pulled it from him.

Lily shivered. *Awful*. She hoped the memory would not live inside her for a long time, but she suspected she'd have to endure that particular awfulness forever.

Hoss cleared his throat, "I promised Bun I'd give you a message when I gave you your Christmas present."

"Oh? Okay. Maybe you better tell me before we get home. Is it something Mama and Papa need to hear?"

Hoss pulled to the side of the road to deliver Bun's message. When she nodded understanding he pulled the car back onto the street.

Hoss refused to go into the Flowers house after he'd helped her to the porch with the crying infants. He left the baby buggy resting at the front steps.

Lily heaved a sigh of relief when she stepped inside the house. "Safe at last." Her mind screamed the thought.

"Oh little Dom. What kind of Christmas will this be?" She murmured against the side of the baby boy's face. "Your dad is one scary man."

"Their buggy's at the front steps, Papa."

Her dad took both babies and stared intently at Lily. "Is the story about you and Dom true?"

"Oh, you've heard already?"

"Drumright is a small town. Everyone knows everything, hon." He handed the babies to their grandmother in her rocker. She murmured and sang to the infants who twittered contentment.

Blackie leaned closer to Lily to whisper. "Dom is up in Dr. Starr's office. His nurse, Maude, is helping to cover his back with some kinda salve. They are also taking off strips of burnt skin." He paused as if waiting for her reaction.

"He was beating a woman, Papa, and I think he was going to start on Pansy next."

Blackie nodded. "Two men, *strangers*, went into Dr. Starr's office awhile ago." He raised his eyebrows at that statement as if he were wondering whether Lily understood the significance. "Maybe we all need to get out of here." He glanced at her mother. "We need to go without getting anyone upset. Okay, Hon?"

She nodded. "Bun sent word to me about that."

"I got us a wagon at the back door. We just need to see that everything we'll need is loaded."

Blackie looked out the front door then pulled the babies' buggy up and into the house. "Do you need more stuff for them?"

"Blankets, I guess, and caps maybe. It's getting cooler."

"Mama," Blackie took the babies and placed them in the buggy, "Get caps for the babes and several blankets too, please. We're gonna take ourselves a little trip. You two kids lie down on a blanket in the wagon bed."

"Now?" Violet's voice held tears.

"Right now. That means you too, Daisy. Hop to it."

"What about Pansy?" Lily shivered.

"Lily, your sister's made her choice. I guess. We gotta go."

Two barrels and several sacks and boxes of food, a sewing machine, the babies in their buggy, a pile of blankets, Mama's rocker, Papa's rifle and a couple of lanterns filled the back of the wagon.

"You and Mama ride in the back with the kids. Hunch down until we get a mile or so out."

"Where are we going?"

"Oilton, Bun bought a place there with a house on it and he told me we could move in there."

"Yeah. He sent word to me, too. I just didn't quite understand. Now I know exactly what he meant."

"Jack Ary and some of his boys are keeping up with the strangers so they warned me." Her Papa whipped up the two horses.

The long miles to Oilton passed in fits of sleep and baby care. Her father refused to let Lily take his place at the reins. The horses were reduced to slow trudging long before they passed the *Oilton* sign.

At the house just at the eastern edge of the busy little oil boom town, they were happy to find beds, chairs, a table, even a gas stove.

Lily spread blankets on a bed in the back bedroom and she and the babies slept. Violet and Daisy raced out to play in the field south of the house.

Blackie put the wagon and the horses in the barn and he spread blankets on the bed in the front bedroom, then he slept too, his wife by his side.

Neither Lily nor her father woke to hear Bun come in the back door during the late afternoon. He brought a man with him. The two men sat at the table to wait. Bun smiled and put a gold ring on the table between them.

"I'm ready," he said. "And I bet Lily is too." His friend nodded and smiled.

When Lily emerged from the bedroom, black hair in wild disarray, she was shocked to see Bun and a stranger in the house.

"Oh, let me clean up." She excused herself to walk toward the bucket of water on a shelf. "Excuse me just a moment." She took the bucket toward the back bedroom.

"Put on your pretty yellow dress, Hon. I like that one 'specially."

"Okay." Lily disappeared into the room where she had been sleeping. She set the bucket on the floor and glanced at the children. Still sound asleep. After washing she swept her long, black hair up, then pulled on the yellow voile hanging in the closet. How did my dress get here? Her work dress hung in the closet. She hung up the everyday brown dress she'd just removed and hung it also. "Looks like I live here." She said aloud as she turned to go back to Bun and his friend.

"Lily, you are the prettiest thing I've seen in a long time." He held out his hand to whirl her in a circle. "Better wake your Mama and Daddy, your little sisters and the twins. We're going to have us a party here."

"Bun, you haven't even introduced your friend." Lily felt heat rising in her cheeks, "Stop being silly." She couldn't help a trill of laughter.

He pulled her close to himself and whispered.

"Marry me, sweet Lily."

"Marry?"

"Let's have a wedding, hon, yours and mine."

"You want to marry me?"

Bun bowed slightly, lifted his hand toward the stranger at the table and made the introduction.

"This is Brother Acton, First Baptist Church, Oilton."

Lily looked at the preacher. "Hello Brother Acton. Are you willing to marry us?"

He nodded then pointed toward the ring on the table.

"Oh Bundy, is that for me?"

"Uh huh, makes everything right and legal."

"Did you talk to Papa?"

"He wants us to marry. He thinks you need my protection."

"Bun, are you sure you want to marry a woman who murdered her brother–in–law?" Lily looked at the floor. "I'm a killer."

Bun took her hand. "In that case, hon, you better marry a killer. That's me, too. The difference between us and really bad people, we've both killed to protect the young, or elderly or helpless."

He bent to put strong arms around Lily.

"Honey, let's just call ourselves 'protectors.' Are you willing to do that?"

"Can we do that?"

"Neither of us wants to hurt anyone but, when some of the police *are* the bad guys then protectors are needed. Let's just get married and try to put all the ugliness behind us."

"Do you love me?"

"Yeah. I've been thinking about this for a long time. I'll have the wife I want and a built-in family." He laughed. "I'll even adopt the twins if you want."

"Adopt?"

"Yeah. Guess you know they're orphans now?"

"Dom?"

"Dead in Starr's office, Maude told me."

"What about the two strangers who are looking for me?"

"Both dead. Jack Ary said someone saw to that."

"And Pansy?"

"In that big green Buick on her way to Tulsa, I heard."

"She left without her babies?" Lily felt a twinge of pain. It was if she'd never really known her favorite sister.

"Hon, Pansy made her choice years ago when she hooked up with that bastard, Dom." He pulled Lily close and pressed her head against his chest. "She doesn't want the twins. She knows you'll take care of them. She's looking around for a new life in a big town which offers big oil bucks, one way or another." He nodded. "We'll all start new right here in lovely little Oilton. Plenty of crooks here, but mostly home grown, like the Doolins and the Daltons, the Terrels and the Hulseys, not to mention the Kimes boys. But no Mafia, hon." He led Lily toward the table where the preacher sat and where the gold ring still rested.

"Let's make a new family here, Brother Acton. Okay?"

Acton stood and asked, "How about the front room? It's big and empty. Everyone can stand while we have the ceremony. Call in all the Mosses, sir."

Lily knocked on the door of the front bedroom. Bun headed to the back to call Lily's sisters in. They came happily when they were told they could each hold one of the twins.

Lily took a deep breath and slipped her hand into the hand of Bundy Moss. Brother Acton faced the smiling pair.

"Dearly beloved, we are gathered together today to witness the joining of this man and this woman in holy matrimony."

The preacher's voice continued, bellowing as if reassuring them all, each of his words echoing loudly enough to quiet the one cow and the many horses in the barn before he came, finally, to the most important part. "I now pronounce you man and wife. You may kiss the bride!"

Bundy did that and Lily, though a bit shy, realized she had loved every moment of the making of their own family.

"Nothing like receiving a new home and a whole new family for Christmas," Lily Moss whispered to her new husband. She stood on tiptoe and pulled Bun's head down until their lips met again.

Note From The Author

This is totally a work of fiction even though many of the names and places in my story were real names and places back in the oil boom days. I wasn't there, but I've heard a great deal about many of those real names and real places.

Peggy Moss Fielding

Printed in the United States
151291LV00005B/1/P